C000161205

CHAPTER 1

I long for the days when I wore my brother's riding breeches instead of the inconvenient gowns my mother forces upon me. Today, I chose not to complain since she reluctantly agreed that I may accompany my father and brother to Saint David's. I ignored the creases across her forehead demonstrating her displeasure as I mounted the frost-colored mare. My father moved to face her, placed his two large hands on her cheeks and kissed her forehead lightly, replacing the worry with a smile on her pale face.

"Your concern need not be wasted on the child," he said. "She has the blood of the Welsh, where women were as fierce a warrior as men. There is no harm in a royal princess experiencing the traditions of her ancestors."

"My worry isn't dedicated to her fierceness, it is that she may never learn to run a proper household," my mother said.

"There will be time enough for needle work and gossip in her future," he said, mounting his light brown warhorse. "Today, we ride."

I moved the reins slightly, signaling my palfrey to the left of my father, while my brother Gruffydd took his place on the right. I didn't look back to my mother, knowing she was shaking her head in disapproval. My brother winked at me with his bright blue eyes. He looked like a fresh version of our father, except father stood a foot taller with aged battle-worn skin and a white scar across his cleft chin. Father was quite handsome with his wide forehead, long narrow nose, and long blonde curls hanging to his shoulders.

Gruffydd was not full-grown, so it was hard for me to

imagine him as a king. He looked too soft, with pale skin like mine, and the same few freckles sprinkled across his nose. I resembled my mother's people of Powys, rather than my father's of Deheubarth. The Welsh were a proud people resisting the influences of the forces outside our borders, but Wales was a fractured country inside its borders, barely held together by the alliances made through treaties and strategic marriages.

My father and mother's marriage was a strategic alliance but their devotion to each other was not forced. My father often said the gods looked favorably on him, since he was forced to marry a goddess. I hoped my marriage to Owain of Powys would be as satisfying as that of my parents.

I always look forward to the journey to Saint David's this time of year. It was the first magical days of spring, when the world awoke from the winter's darkness and the torrential rains loosened the rich soil so the bulbs could relax and let go of their bonds allowing fields of yellow daffodils mixed with carpets of bluebells, filling the air with a sweet freshness that I took in with every breath. I imagined this is where the fairies gathered to drink sweet wine from their bright yellow cups, wearing tiny blue flowers in their hair.

The road twisted through the forest and the sun was filtered by a canopy of trees, the new fronds of the ferns reached out like tentacles to welcome us with their thick, green blanket and the new leaves of the giant oaks danced to the songs of the goldfinch.

The closer we got to Saint David's, the more travelers we met along the road, many who were making a pilgrimage to the cathedral. My father paid good silver to travelers that could provide any useful information along the way. My father said we must heed what is said because it's the hungry and discontented that can bring down a country faster than the largest army.

Our arrival caused the usual commotion as the villagers gathered, eager to see their well-loved King, my father, King Rhys of Deheubarth. My brother and I were also well received. As the only children of Rhys and Gwladys, our existence provided security to our country. My brother would be the next king, and my betrothal to Prince Owain would secure the continued alliance with the Kingdom of Powys. These were promises made to God at our birth, and we were bound to them as an angel is bound to heaven.

We arrived as the sun was directly above our heads. The yard was crowded with foreigners and noblemen, some I recognized, and some were strangers. The colors and languages that surrounded me were a source of excitement, and I could hardly sit still. Just being here in the middle of things made me feel a part of the bigger world. Bishop Rhygyfarch greeted our entourage, along with a few English priests who seemed to be infiltrating the local churches and abbeys more and more. I'm sure this particular group gathered here today were hoping to convince the English King to loosen his purse strings and increase funding for their individual parishes.

Each group gathered flew their banners indicating their house or kingdom. The bright sun reflected the colors, making the whole scene even more exciting. Our banners were bright red with a large yellow dragon. I looked around until I spotted the dark blue banners with the two golden lions of the English King.

The English King's retinue was handsomely dressed in dark blue tunics trimmed in gold brocade. The guards stood round the King and were scattered through the courtyard for security. As we approached, the crowded courtyard parted like the Red Sea, allowing our small procession to move across the field, closing ranks behind us as we exited the other side where King William flanked by what must be two of his four sons, acknowledged our approach with a slight nod.

My father and brother dismounted, and I patiently waited for my brother's assistance when an unexpected foreign hand reached out and touched mine causing me to jump in surprise.

"I'm so sorry to scare you, my lady," a young man said as he smiled up at me.

Not knowing how to take such a bold advance, I looked toward my father for some guidance, but he and my brother were already distracted by the King. With reluctance, I accepted the hand, and before I knew it, two hands around my waist easily lifted me off my horse and gently set me on the fresh field grass. The closeness of the stranger disturbed me, although it was obvious, he was a member of the royal party. I could feel the warmth of his breath on my cheek. Although a good head shorter than my father, his strength was impressive. Standing face to face, I was frozen in place and tongue-tied as I looked into the bright blue eyes that matched the royal blue cape draping his left shoulder. The pin that held his cape indicated he also was in the royal family.

"Princess Nesta of Deheubarth," he said confidently, as he took a knee in front of me, took my hand in his, and gently kissed it. The warmth of his lips moved from the back of my hand directly to the center of my heart.

"A bard's tribute has hardly captured reality, as I can now see for myself there are no comparisons. Even if I could describe the shape of a perfect rose, the brightness of a star on a moonless night, or the first breath of morning, I could not find words to match the beauty standing before me."

I felt my face turn hot as he smiled like a stable cat who had just caught a royal mouse. His hair was as black as a raven's wing, cut to frame his perfect face. I had to remember to breathe, careful to conceal my discomfort.

"Prince Henry, at your service," he said, not letting go of my hand. Henry was the fourth son of the King and the most notorious in rumors that have reached all the way to Deheubarth.

"I am pleased to meet you," I said, pulling my hand back just as Gruffydd arrived and moved to create space between us as he reached his hand toward Henry, forcing me to step back as he filled the space. The two shook hands but Henry's eyes didn't leave mine until I was completely blocked by my brother.

"Henry," Gruffydd said, "I see you have escaped Bishop Osmund's curriculum."

"Apparently, my destiny was waiting for me here," he said, smiling past my brother as if still speaking to me even though I now stood a few paces away.

"I thought the clergy was in your future," Gruffydd said.

"A mother's wish for her fourth son, but it seems my talent with numbers has secured my position as protector of the King's fortune. I have accepted the treasury post, so I expect to find my way down these roads often." He laughed, almost too loudly, catching the attention of nearby men, including that of my father, who by the look on his face was not too pleased. With a nod to Bishop Rhygyfarch, he turned back to his conversation with the King.

The Bishop understood my father's silent command and was soon at my side, artfully leading me away from Henry and toward the massive cathedral. As we walked away, I felt an unreasonable longing; I fought the urge to look back but knew the young Prince was fully aware of my direction.

It wasn't long that my senses returned, and the allure of the raven-haired prince was replaced by the grandeur of the largest cathedral in all of Wales. No matter how many times I walked in the shadow of these walls, I had to remind myself to breathe.

Saint David's was a magnificent representation of Christianity, created by the Celtic Christian patron who founded it as a secluded monastery. No matter how often I visited, its effect on me was breathtaking. Known as the holiest place outside of Rome, the cathedral attracts pilgrims from lands both near and far. Some, including King William, believe two pilgrimages a year to Saint David's is equal to a pilgrimage to Rome.

Saint David's is a well-known sacred destination in a strategic location, as it sits on the southwest bank of the Irish Sea, holding much of the church's fortune and many important relics. The place where treaties are signed and payments collected, including the annual tribute paid by my father to secure peace in our ancestral lands and maintain Welsh rule.

While this arrangement was in effect, our lands were safe from an English invasion. The English King recognized my father's talents in negotiating with the leaders of unstable lands in Wales. He was satisfied enough with the small fortune he collected from my father that he didn't often interfere in our Welsh traditions and officially recognized my father, Rhys ap Tewdwr, as the rightful King of Wales. Feeling unfairly treated, some of our cousins ruling other Welsh lands were openly hostile to us but didn't dare make an enemy of the English King.

The Bishop and I walked silently down the path. His steps were so short that I had difficulty matching his stride without tripping over my own toes, and our short walk to the side garden seemed to take forever. We were obviously killing time until the men were seated at the long table for the midday meal. Some traditions just couldn't be challenged, but it made no sense to me to seat ladies last.

The garden was beautiful, and the scents were overwhelming. The rhododendrons were just starting to bloom, green buds teasing us with bright pink tips soon to bloom into large pink flowers providing their sweetness to the fresh spring air.

We sat on a stone bench artfully set in a small alcove, surrounded by a carpet of purple and pink impatiens and a curtain of thick green ivy supported by an iron trellis above our heads. On the bench, I became my six-year-old self, seated next to my father at this very same bench where he told me stories of his childhood and the grandmother I was named after.

This was also the place where I sat many times to mourn my small brother, Hywell, lost shortly before his fifth birthday. I could still see him running through the tall grass and hear the echoes of his uninhibited laughter. I was lost in these memories when the Bishop broke the silence.

"Is your mother well?" he asked.

"Very well," I said. "She has been busy with her garden. I'm afraid the weeds have a stronger will than her flowers. She says it's a battle she must fight every day."

"I'm afraid there will always be a battle for this rich Welsh soil, whether it be man or mayweed," he said resolutely as he stood up.

"I'll credit it to all the blood shed that enriches it so," I said.

"My lady should not dwell on the past," the Bishop said offering his small hand.

"If we ignore the past, it will surely find its way back," I said repeating words I'd heard from my father many times. I accepted his hand and again stood next to him as he shook his head in disapproval.

"Faith in God will deliver us," he said, keeping my hand in his as we walked at the same slow speed as before.

"Deliver us from what?" I asked.

The Bishop stopped and faced me—his eyes were a cloudy gray and couldn't quite focus as he spoke. I couldn't tell if I had said something wrong.

"The past cannot protect you. Your ancestors provide you strength and direction, but your choices are of free will and those choices will dictate your future and your children's future. Make those decisions for yourself, young Nesta, and you will live with pain and heartache; make them for God and you will live in peace."

"What about all the gods of the past, are they gone?"

"Do not speak of such things. There is only one God now," the Bishop looked around nervously.

"I don't understand," I said.

"You cannot change things from the outside; you must fit in modern times to be able to influence the world. Just remember as you travel in the space above us that even the son of God came not to be served but to serve and to give his life as a ransom for many."

I still didn't understand but was willing to keep silent, keeping his words close but also distracted by my own thoughts as we continued to walk the path until we reached the back entrance to the dining hall.

CHAPTER 2

The weight of the room was so heavy on me, I could barely eat a bite of the thick lamb stew and freshly baked braided bread that I had been craving since the horses were saddled this morning. The men's deep chatter rumbled in my ears like a stampede of wild horses. My focus was not on the men who dipped the thick bread into their trenches leaving trails of gravy, devouring the stew as if they hadn't eaten in a week. Instead, I was busy stealing side glances of the young prince sitting directly across from me. On more than one occasion I was caught suffering the sly smile as he recognized my attention. I tried to watch how his mouth moved as he spoke and memorize the timbre of his voice as he spoke easily of politics and foreign affairs. I noticed he also studied my movements and paid attention as I spoke politely to the woman who sat beside me. His attention made me uncomfortable and it took everything I had to maintain my composure.

After the meal, my brother escorted me back to the garden. Gruffydd knew Saint David's well as he had spent most of his youth amongst its books and scrolls. My brother's education was provided by the Bishop himself, who often remarked on Gruffydd's extraordinary instinct for learning, especially when it came to mathematics and writing. I was similarly eager for learning and was educated by the nuns at Carew Abbey well past the usual requirements for young women, but my father's tolerance of my will often overruled my mother's wishes.

"I would like to witness the King's business someday," I said.

"My darling girl, it's all just politicking and stories of wars past. You would be tormented by boredom. I'm sure you could find some better use of your time. You should have stayed with mother and continued your lessons." Gruffydd smiled at me like I was a child under his protection even as I was older. He should have realized that I was not one of the maidens under his spell. His disarming smile was wasted on me. I would continue to do what I pleased when I pleased as he well knew. We had spent most of our childhood together, kept apart from other children and the rest of the world for our protection. We spent so much time together, we could read each other's most private thoughts. But now that Gruffydd was spending more and more time away at my father's side, I was feeling isolated and alone. I would gladly suffer boredom to be included in their activities.

"Would you deny me an experience that could only add value to my knowledge of world affairs? I promise not to be a bother." I blinked my blue eyes several times and pouted my lips, a simple but effective technique I used on the two men in my family.

"And further expose you to the eyes of these men?" Gruffydd shook his head defiantly. "Wars have been started for less." I pretended to be naïve to his implications, but his expression told me he was serious. "Furthermore, the Archbishop would never allow it."

"Women have no use in the Christian world except to marry and produce heirs."

"Nesta! Stop this blasphemy, we are not free in our opinions. We are not children anymore and we are not free to speak as we wish. You are not a common woman, which may be your misfortune if you cannot control the warrior inside you."

"You are correct that I am not a common woman. I inherited this soul from my ancestors and when I am married, my husband will value my opinions and consult me on matters important to our country. Both my sons and daughters will be valuable in ruling the lands they inherit."

"You have always had a warrior's heart, but I fear your life will be a disappointment if you don't accept the world, we live in. Your life is not your own. You are a servant to our people."

I felt my blood boiling through my body every time we had this conversation. If I had been born a son rather than a daughter, I would have freedom and could travel the country, making a real difference. Instead, I must find solace in making decisions of great importance like the color of thread I will use on a tapestry.

Gruffydd, hoping to change the subject and ease the tension, now found the distraction he had sought worse than the ire of his sister. Prince Henry appeared and stood between us.

"Nesta, Princess of Deheubarth." Henry bowed toward me and turned on his heels toward my brother. "Prince Gruffydd."

Both young men were of similar age and both sons of kings, but Henry seemed to believe his position superior, even though Gruffydd would inherit the crown of our father while Henry, as the fourth son, would probably end up a duke somewhere in England or Normandy. The standoff reminded me of two young bucks bending their heads and touching horns to establish dominance.

Gruffydd stood tall and intimidating. He was a proud Welshman, well known for his expertise with a longbow. He smiled politely at Henry, disguising his loathing of the Normans who caused our family constant distress by silently threatening our borders with hostile takeover. *Maintaining the current peace,* our father said, *was a delicate balancing act.*

Having spent time together on various occasions, Henry took advantage of Gruffydd's main weakness. "I hear there is a lively game of knucklebones across the yard," Henry said. Gruffydd's resolute expression changed instantly as Henry nodded his head toward the northeast corner of the stables where several young men had gathered in an alcove. The group stood in a typical half-circle, some kneeling, others bent over. Gruffydd gazed across the yard, eager to join the game.

"I'm sure there is room for one more," Henry said, watching Gruffydd.

Gruffydd reached into his pocket and fingered what was likely at least one pair of dice. He looked at me as he weighed his oath to my father that he would keep his eye on me against the laughter and cheers of the dice throwers.

"Go," I said gently. Gruffydd looked at me and then at Henry. He shook his head in disappointment, looking toward the group once again.

"I vow on my father's crown, Prince Gruffydd, that I will keep your sister under my protection." Gruffydd rolled his eyes at Henry's pledge, but still decided that there was no harm in leaving me in the care of this young man. Gruffydd knew I could take care of myself, but this time he may have underestimated my resolve.

"I'm afraid you have found my brother's weakness," I said.

"It's the weakness of most men our age. I would probably find myself in the center of it, if I didn't have such a beautiful distraction," he said with a smile.

"You are welcome to join," I said. "I am perfectly able to entertain myself."

"I may have done that, had I not arranged the game myself to lure your brother away so I may learn more of the beautiful Nesta of Deheubarth."

As he moved toward me. I watched his eyes as they moved from my eyes to my full breasts, recently beginning to push the limits of my bodice. I suddenly felt self-conscious and resisted the urge to cover my cleavage. I took a deep breath and stood straight as if I really was a confident Welsh woman.

"I'll admit that was a clever move," I said, and walked past the prince, taking control of the situation. Henry took the hint, matched my stride, and took his place to the left of me. I had no idea where I was leading him, but if I hadn't taken some action I would have been caught in his web. Now, I had some control.

"Why, may I ask, would such a lady as yourself attend such a dull meeting as this?" Henry asked.

"Had I stayed home, I would have enjoyed a day filled with meaningless gossip and discussions of what gown to wear to the next court event."

"You don't enjoy court events?"

"I want to know about the real world. I want to have adventures of my own. My father allows me to have opinions and to discuss politics and the business of our land," I said firmly.

"I see." Henry stopped suddenly and turned toward an elaborate statue of an Italian cross. He put his hand to his chin, and I wondered if he was listening to me.

"He even asks my advice on occasion," I said softly. My father had never actually asked my opinion but did tolerate my constant questions and opinions. My mother, conversely, believed such tolerance inappropriate.

I waited a few impatient minutes while Henry seemed distracted, then asked, "What are you thinking? Do you not believe me? Were you even listening?" I sounded like a child begging for attention. Henry slowly turned toward me and smiled. His handsome face and blue eyes entrancing.

"You, Lady Nesta, have my full attention," he said. "I have memorized every word you have uttered, both the content and the sound of your voice as you spoke."

I was shocked into silence. This man's words were those I would have spoken, encouraging me that this was meant to be.

"I'll admit, I've never met a woman more interesting or as beautiful. I am pleasantly surprised that there is much more to you than what is on the surface." He turned back to the Italian cross and reached out to touch the jewels inlaid in the statue.

"Like this cross. There are many with similar form." He pointed at other crosses that littered the property. "But this one is unique in that it has been embellished by the most expensive jewels in the world. Each time this cathedral has been sacked, this cross has been ignored because, I assume, the thieves believed it inlaid with common glass. The truth is that this cross is the most valuable piece at Saint David's, maybe in all of Wales, likely only surpassed by the collection of artifacts kept deep in the vaults in Rome. The rubies, emeralds, and jade are not only genuine but of uncommon size."

"I had no idea," I said. I had walked past it many times before, but now looked at the cross anew. The jewels were imbedded deeply, leaving only their vague shapes exposed.

"It's now the first secret we share," he said.

"Why does it need to be a secret?" I asked.

"In order to save it from those who would tear it apart, we must let it continue to hide in plain sight." He turned to me and moved close to whisper in my ear. "Like you, my dear Nesta, who hides her jewels in plain sight. Be careful who you expose your secrets to."

"I have no secrets," I whispered back, for no apparent reason, since we were far from any others. He watched my lips as I softly said, "You confuse me, Henry."

Henry just smiled and took my arm, leading me further down the path until the front lawn was in full view. He signaled to his groom, who quickly brought his tall black warhorse.

"Please." Henry signaled me towards the beast. He didn't give me a chance to speak but lifted me to the stirrup where I could climb atop. Before I even settled, I felt Henry's firm body pressing against my back. His arms reached tightly around me as he pulled the reigns signaling the horse into a gallop away from the cathedral to a narrow path through the woods.

"Am I being kidnapped?" I asked, with no thoughts of propriety or responsibilities, just the thrill of being a girl swept away.

"I vow no harm will come to you, Lady Nesta. Consider me your protector. If you are ever kidnapped, I will declare war to save you," he said, patting my thigh before leaving his hand to rest there.

I felt suddenly afraid, not of Henry, but of my own will. I closed my eyes and let the air cool my skin. I forced myself to calm down as Henry slowed the horse and trotted us into a small clearing where the only sounds were from a stream running through the center, narrow enough to step over. The sun was still high above our heads, providing filtered light through the thick canopy of the trees above. It was as if we were on a great stage surrounded by an audience of small firs, and the sounds of the birds mixed with the water running over the large stones was the music. Henry took the small blanket from his horse's back and laid it in the center of the moss-covered ground.

"Will you not be missed this afternoon?" I asked.

"If we are gone too long, perhaps," he said, "but the Archbishop's recordings will take hours. My only duty is to determine how much tribute is due and to ensure the collections are accurate. I have fulfilled the first and will recount before I transport the chest back to the castle."

"How do you determine the tribute?" I asked.

"This is the business of the king, my dear. I cannot disclose such information. For all I know, you could be a spy," Henry said teasingly.

"A spy you say. Hardly, for what I know is obvious. When people have food in their belly and a fire in their hearth, they have no appetite for uprising and are willing to pay a tribute to a king who ensures that peace. But if the tribute is too high—"

Before I could finish, Henry had his lips firmly pressed to mine. His hands held my face, and his tongue explored my mouth. Unsure how to respond to my body's reaction to this new experience, I followed his lead. He laid me on the ground, and I couldn't catch my breath. I sat up flushed and on the verge of tears. My emotions ran wild, my mind overflowed with thoughts of loyalty and promises mixed with passion and desire.

"I can't do this," I said softly, as a tear ran down my cheek. Henry wiped it away with his thumb.

"It was just a kiss," he said.

"It's now the second secret we must keep," I said. "I am promised to another."

"It seems you have the weight of the world on your beautiful shoulders." He put his hands on my waist and looked into my eyes. Then he again softly kissed my lips.

"My responsibilities extend beyond this moment," I said.

"As do mine," he said. "But I cannot help but imagine a world where the two of us could find a way to be together. To rule together."

"You imagine a fantasy, for the fourth son of a king to marry another king's daughter who is promised to another."

"Dear Lady, I live in a world where anything is possible. The very moment I saw you, I nearly fell from my horse. When you trusted me to help you dismount, I felt great things could happen."

I allowed Henry to gently push me to the ground. He kissed the exposed part of my breasts. He moved his lips from there to my neck until his hot breath was behind my ear. I let out a small moan. He paused to consider my response and decided it was an invitation that was as I didn't stop him as he pulled the laces, freeing my breasts.

I had no experience to prepare myself for such a situation as this except my own imagination. My dreams included the touch of a man such as this, but the opportunity was never a reality. I knew I needed to resist but my body only responded leaving my head in the clouds. If the rustling of the forest hadn't broken the spell, Henry might have conquered Wales that day.

I had just enough time to lace my bodice back in place and was leaning over the small steam splashing cold water on my hot cheeks before Gruffydd arriving at the clearing holding the reins of my horse. Henry had already returned the blanket to his horse's back. I hid my face from his glare, fearing he would read my guilt.

"Any luck at the bones?" Henry asked Gruffydd, attempting to take the focus off of me while I composed myself.

"Pennies lost and pennies gained, but my pockets feel a bit heavier than they were this morn," Gruffydd said to Henry as he handed me the reins. With Henry's silent assistance, I mounted my horse and took the position next to my brother. Henry smiled as he mounted his own horse and took the lead on the return path. I didn't look directly at my brother, but I could see at a glance that his jaw was clenched with displeasure. For the first time, I wished my brother, and I were not so close.

Gruffydd slowed until there was enough distance between us that Henry could not overhear, he turned his face to me and in a low voice warned me. "Nesta, you must never confess your actions to anyone, or that I left you unattended today. Father will not approve of your close acquaintance with this Norman, whose very existence threatens our rule."

"We are only friendly to keep the peace," I said defiantly, swallowing my tears.

"You are not free to make your own decisions," he said loudly enough that Henry slowed and turned toward us. My brother's fury was a flame that could quickly burn out of control, so I decided to keep silent, and looked down in shame.

"You belong to Wales and your children will ride beside me, protecting our lands against all others," he said through gritted teeth pointing ahead, "likely this very man and his children."

I watched Henry ahead and as if he knew our conversation, signaled his horse into a gallop, increasing the distance between us until he was out of sight. He understood it would look better if we were not seen being led out of the woods by my brother. I appreciated his concern for my reputation but watching him go caused a pain I did not expect.

"Nesta, this man and his charms are not worth the price," Gruffydd said reading my mind.

"I don't know what came over me," I said. "I was carried away by the possibility of a different life than the one prescribed for me before I was born. For the first time, I felt in control." I wasn't certain my words reached his ears, but as I said them, I realized he was right. There was only one destiny for me, and I needed to put Henry out of my mind.

CHAPTER 3

My resolve to keep Henry from my thoughts became difficult as he regularly visited Deheubarth as the King's representative. Henry was to determine the tribute due to the crown.

"It's the beginning of winter and I must measure the stores as the collections were based on estimates," Henry explained his arrival on a fine summer day. The weather was light as were the spirits of the men. Father was once again away settling a dispute between the Welsh Lords and the English. The latter continued to build castles either encroaching on Welsh land or so close to the border that when the sheep and pigs got loose, the Welsh landowners would claim them as their own. Today, the dispute was between two Welshmen on fishing rights so again he was conveniently away for Henry's visit.

"What if the harvest was less than the estimates, do they receive the tax back?" I asked guilty of the excitement I felt as he moved close.

"No man overestimates his crops. I assure you; he holds back enough for this day. They expect the additional tax. It is just how it works." I watched Henry turn pages and make marks in his book. His face serious with concentration.

Finally, Henry closed the book and looked at me carefully.

"Come closer," he said softly reaching his hand to me. I took it and let him pull me close. He kissed my breast before standing to face me. I could not resist this man and his words and let myself melt into his arms.

"I have an important question," he said pulling back enough to look at my face," Nesta, you are my weakness, I cannot fall asleep without thinking you should be next to me. I wake in the morning aching to see your face. I'm afraid I cannot live without you."

"You are wishing for an event that will never come to be. Our destinies exist apart."

"They don't have to, my dear. I want to marry you."

"I feel the same, but my father will never allow it," I said letting the possibilities seep in.

"Do you love me?" Henry put his lips near my ear and whispered the words again, "do you love me?"

"I do love you."

"Then it is settled, we will marry." He kissed me on the lips and I again melted to his touch. He reached around my waist and pulled me into him, and I could feel his hardness. He continued to kiss me until he noticed my resolve and laid me down on a nearby pallet in the storage shed and lifted my skirt. He removed his own shirt exposing his defined chest.

I softly touched him as he laid on top of me kissing me as he did. I was taken away as he found me under my skirt, and I could feel his arousal near on my thigh. I switched from excitement to fear and back again before it was no longer a choice and Henry entered me in a single force causing me to cry out.

That seemed to relieve him as a smile crossed his face and he kept the rhythm of his stokes until the initial pain ceased and I could feel the change in my soul as a small tear escaped from the corner of my eye as I realized nothing would ever be the same.

It was his release that surprised me the most with its dramatic finish. He made a sound like a horse whose hoof was stuck in the muck. He rolled off me and I pushed my skirt down. He looked pleased with himself as he kissed my cheek before sitting up.

"When will you speak with your father about our marriage?" I asked hoping to gain back some sense of normalcy as the ache between my legs lingered.

"I'm not worried about my father. He hasn't picked a wife

for me. It's your father I worry about, but I think that problem has been solved. Your betrothed is no longer a worthy candidate for marriage."

"Owain?"

"He has fled to Ireland. His father, Cadwygan, has agreed to negotiate with my father for his return but it is unlikely Cadwygan will agree to the terms."

"What did he do?"

"He attacked an English castle at the eastern border of Powys. My father has rescinded the peace treaty with his father and has taken his lands of Gwynedd from him. If Cadwygan makes any attempts to take Deheubarth, my father will take Powys too. There is no longer a reason to broker a marriage for peace. It's done." I wrapped my arms around him. He held me tightly and kissed me.

"When will you speak with my father?" I asked.

"After my father blesses the union, I will meet with your father. Until then, you must keep our plans close."

For the next few months, Henry's visits continued, and we would make love at every opportunity and I continued to beg him to speak with my father. I craved his touch and felt lost when he wasn't near. His continued promises of marriage but there was always a reason to put it off.

To my relief, my father brought the news of Owain's escape to Ireland.

"How long will he be in exile?" my mother asked my father.

"As long as the King lives, I'm afraid. Owain is an impulsive young man. His father is quite distraught."

"What about Nesta's betrothal?" my mother asked as I remained silently hoping for my release.

"I am sorry, Nesta," he said, "I am not sure what can be done. I can speak with the King on his behalf, but I feel I have no weight in this matter."

"I understand," I said hiding the joy I felt all the way to my toes.

The next morning, my mother came to my chamber to wake me. It was too cold to show my face from under the covers, so she shook me gently, believing that I was still asleep.

"Wake, child," my mother said.

"I'm awake."

"How are you feeling this morning?" she said as she pulled the covers from my head and put her hand on my forehead like I was a child.

"I still feel dizzy when I stand, and when I smell the morning sausage, I need to empty my stomach." She handed me a piece of stale bread and a cup of ale.

"Eat this before you get up. It will help."

"What's wrong with me? I haven't felt well for weeks," I said.

"It's the child," she said. "It's a common symptom."

"Oh mother, no. It's not possible I am with child," I said, looking at my mother in a panic, at the same time realizing I hadn't needed the small stack of rags in over a month.

"Not possible is not the same as not expected," she said.

"How did you know?" I asked her.

"A mother always knows," she said petting my head.

"What am I going to do? What is father going to say?"

"I don't know, my dear. I'm afraid you have changed your destiny."

My mother looked sad, and I was sorry to cause her distress, but my emotions quickly transformed from worry to excitement. I was carrying Henry's child in my belly. Now we could be wed and form the alliance we had planned many times during our secret meetings.

"I can't wait to tell Henry," I said.

"You can never make this known," my mother said quickly. "This child is a threat to peace and may cause our people to revolt. We are barely hanging on to our ways as it is."

I knew what she said was true. Although Christianity was the country's official religion, many of the Welsh people held tightly to old traditions. The bishops at Saint David's, who had not been replaced by the English, turned a blind eye to the ancient practices. Even at a church burial, people could perform Celtic rituals if they weren't too obvious.

"Maybe this child can represent peace between nations," I said.

"I can't imagine how."

"I don't see why this child cannot bind us. Father has said many times, 'When the old ways and the new ways collide, there lies an opportunity.' Couldn't this child be the stability between nations? If we can show such a union is in the best interest of the people, they will support it."

"You sound more like a statesman than the mother of a bastard," she said. "Your confidence depends on a rational mind while we live in a land where most people are naturally suspicious. Many have lived in a war-torn country most of their lives. This peace we now enjoy is fragile. Chaos is only your friend if you can harness the energy it creates."

"Now you sound more like a statesman than a mother," I said. My stomach twisted and I reached for the basin to empty it again.

"As your mother, I prescribe fresh air. Get dressed. We are going to the village."

I hurried to dress. Several times I put my hand on my belly and wondered what the child would look like. If it was a boy, would it favor Henry?

As we reached the outskirts of our castle walls, we rode side-by-side through one of the large wooden doors. The guards removed the side plank as we approached and stood aside as we moved through. The village surrounded the outer castle walls and extended to the edge of the forest. Identical small wooden shacks that had been constructed next to each other lined the dirt road promoting their wares. The smell of baking shops filled the air with the sweet smell of meat pies and dried fish. My stomach, still a little weak, craved fermented cider over the food.

The villagers greeted us pleasantly as we rode along the

main road. Though the day was cold, the snow and rain held off, and crowds were larger than usual. We dismounted and released our horses to our steward.

My mother caught sight of her friend entering the candle shop, so we separated and I went in search of cider as she joined her friend. I walked past the vegetable carts loaded with potatoes, carrots, and squash. Winter vegetables were not my favorite, but we had plenty of apples and walnuts to add variety to our meals. I spotted a stall with a keg of cider across the street but as I started to cross, I noticed two children in an alley rolling around, fists flying, and covered in mud.

I saw that one of the children was a girl, and the other a boy who currently had a fistful of her bright red hair pushing her face toward the ground. I rushed to the wrestling match and grabbed the young boy's arm just before he pushed her head into a puddle of rocks and mud.

"Stop!" I ordered.

Both children froze and they looked up at me. Somehow, they seemed familiar but I wasn't sure how. They both looked at me but with more like curiosity than familiarity. The boy had a long scar that ran from above his right eye at an angle across his face until it disappeared under his chin. His dark eyes were blank and seemed to stare through me while the girl tilted her head and watched my every move through tear filled eyes.

I reached out to pull him up, but he rose and pushed me so hard that I fell backwards and sat in the mud next to the girl. Before I could react, the boy fled through the alley and disappeared around the corner.

The girl's mop of red hair was full of mud. She tried to brush the tears from her cheeks but only smeared more mud onto her face. I offered a corner of my cloak which she silently refused. I insisted, and as I cleaned off the mud and tears, I saw that she wasn't as young as I had thought, maybe just a few years younger than I was. Her body was covered with cuts and bruises, and she held her arm like it was hurt.

"Why was that boy attacking you?" I asked, but she just

stared at me.

"Do you understand me?" I repeated the phrase in Welsh, English, and French but the girl still did not respond.

"I can't help you if you don't tell me where you live or what happened to you," I said, even though she probably didn't understand me. Just then, a stray cat jumped from the roof of the nearby shop to the ground between us causing me to step back in surprise. The girl took the distraction as an opportunity to escape and ran. Without thinking, I followed her as much as I could, finding myself lost after so many twists and turns in the twisted labyrinth of pathways. I should be familiar with these paths but the morning sky had filled with dark clouds, quickly turning day into night, heavy with moisture until the sky released its burden all at once causing me to seek immediate shelter.

Now I was less concerned with finding the girl than with finding my way back from the edges of the village. I stood under the thatched roof of an empty open shop that smelled of wet wool and straw as if it once held some type of animal. As the rain began to subside, I suddenly became aware that I didn't stand alone, a woman bent with age leaning on a staff startled me.

"Fear not, my child. I am also seeking shelter from this," she held her hand to the sky. She looked directly at me with deep-set black eyes and a toothless smile. She then spoke words foreign to my ears.

"I'm afraid I don't understand your words," I said.

Finally, the rain calmed to a light mist.

"Come," she said as she took my hand in hers and I didn't resist. I let her lead me back to the main road.

"Thank you," I said as she reached into a large pocket of her cloak and pulled out a small package tightly wrapped in moss and dried leaves and carefully placed it into my hands.

"Those are the children you left behind. They will return damaged, abandoned for your own ambitions, remember their faces as they will come for you in a shadow life. It is a choice you make, make it wisely."

I didn't understand what she was saying and needed to ask her to repeat what she just said but I was back on the main road just a few blocks from where I started. I looked back to again to the old woman, but she had disappeared.

The shawl I was wearing around my shoulders was soaked so it did nothing to protect me from the cold. I took a few steps and felt dizzy, so I sat on a wooden bench in front of a closed-up shop, hoping my mother might find me there. I was still holding the small package that the old woman had placed in my hands.

People of the village often gave us gifts and it was good luck to accept these gifts with honor. However, as I carefully unwrapped the moss, I recognized the familiar feathers of a bird. The small bird was stiff, its eyes had been gouged out, and it was missing part of one of its dark blue wings. I let out a scream and threw it to the ground. I looked around again for the old woman but only saw an empty street. It was a faraway laugh somewhere behind me that provided the motivation to leave the bench desperate to find my mother.

She was just coming out of a shop, her basket loaded with colored fabrics when I found her and wrapped my arms around her, nearly knocking her to the ground.

"What on earth happened to you?" she asked. I was soaked, covered with mud as tears streamed down my face. "Are you hurt?"

I just shook my head as the tears kept falling.

"I think I've been cursed," I said sobbing.

"Why do you think that?"

"It was an old lady. It was like she knew I would be there."

"Well, let's get you home," she said.

Safely back on my horse next to my mother, I stopped crying and looked back at the village, glad to be leaving it behind. I noticed the boy and girl who were fighting earlier, now standing together watching my departure. The girl was obviously holding something in her hands and before I turned back, the girl lifted her arms and released a small bird from her grip. I ducked as the bird flew right over my head. The bird looked just like the one the old woman had put in my hands except this one was clearly alive. The bird landed on a branch that crossed over the path in front of us. As we passed under the branch, bird excrement dropped on top of the horse's head. The horse barely noticed. But I gasped loudly.

"What is it?" my mother asked.

"The children. They were…I tried…I don't understand," I tried to explain, but couldn't produce the words.

"Calm down, child."

"Am I cursed?"

"Certainly not," she said confidently.

My mother's words were soothing, as I believed she knew more of the old ways than she ever spoke of. She was from the north where Christianity was openly rejected, yet the English continued to build cathedrals and fill them with English bishops.

"She didn't speak our language," I said describing the events in the alley.

"You cannot be cursed unless you allow it. It isn't black magic," she said. "It was meant both as a warning and a blessing."

"I don't understand."

"They probably spoke the old dialect," she said, "A dead bird is a symbol of a misfortune that leads to a path to something much better. You will have to understand each piece in the context of your life to find its meaning."

We finally crossed the small wooden bridge leading to the castle's outer wall and entered through the same wooden door as before. As soon as we got close enough, I spotted Henry's horse drinking from the trough. Both my mother and I dismounted and handed the reins to the groom. I could hardly contain myself, looking to my mother to release me. She nodded, allowing me to go, and I almost ran to look for Henry.

Henry was in the kitchen, seated at the long table. He was talking with the women baking and chewing on fresh bread straight from the oven. When he saw me, he stood with a look of shock on his face. I had forgotten how I must look, covered in mud, and could hardly contain myself. I ran into his arms with no regard for what the staff might think. Henry didn't resist. He just held me tightly as I wept.

"We are having a child," I whispered too loudly in his ear, and everyone in the kitchen froze like statues.

Henry only paused for a moment before lifting me off the ground in excitement. I repeatedly kissed his whole face as he responded enthusiastically. I felt sure he was the love of my life and I was his.

"We have to marry soon," I said, "I want my child legitimate."

"Of course," he said.

Since my father was away, Henry slept in my chamber that evening, not bothering to hide the fact from my mother. She did not approve, but she didn't deny me the comfort of Henry's arms.

CHAPTER 4

Gruffydd's loud screams shook me from a sound sleep. At first, I thought it was just a bad dream but I heard it again accompanied by the hounding echo of his distress, bringing me out of my warm bed and straight to the window. I could see a small crowd forming around the stable doors so I quickly put my cloak on over my shift and ran to the open doors weaving through the people until I saw my brother kneeling over his favorite war horse that lay still on its side, its brown eyes open but lifeless.

Two stable boys stood next to Gruffydd, looking helpless. It was the same black stallion I had ridden to the village a few weeks ago before, now lying dead. Gruffydd looked at me with tears that did not fall and simply shook his head. Gruffydd had this horse since it was a foal. I remember he had to hand-feed it when its mother took ill. This was the horse Gruffydd rode in his first contest but that was years ago and now the beast was used as stud or short trips to the village. Gruffydd wouldn't cry, but seeing his anguish, I could not help but let my tears fall for him. I kissed my brother's cheek and knelt near the poor beast's head and brushed his black mane with my fingers. Gruffydd finally closed the big brown eyes and wiped the bit of white foam that had collected around the horse's mouth with the back of his hand.

I felt sorrow for my brother as he was broken but at the same time, I couldn't help wondering what lives in a man's heart that a beast can bring tears from even the strongest of men but the killing of humans in war seems to have little effect. It is in that moment I noticed a white smear on top of the horse's head. It looked like the remnants of bird droppings, in the same spot where the bird hit my horse a few weeks ago. A chill ran down my spine, and I tried to dismiss this as a strange coincidence. I said a silent prayer for the poor dead horse and for my brother's sorrow but I couldn't shake the memories of the old woman's curse.

For the next few weeks, Gruffydd kept to himself and my mother was busy with the household while my father was away. I had not heard from Henry for over a month and I was convinced that he had either changed his mind or his father forbade our union. But while I longed for Henry, I dreaded seeing my father, who would soon see the obvious changes in my body.

The early morning mist was like a soft blanket of clouds that had fallen from heaven and settled on earth. The sounds of morning were dull and muted by the thickness of the air, but I could hear familiar voices across the courtyard. I looked through my window and saw it was my father and his contingent coming through the gates.

Gruffydd had mounted and rode out to greet the party as they returned. Normally, Gruffydd would have been alongside my father but there was some rumor of a disturbance in the nearby village so he was left to protect our walls.

I could see my brother and father stopped near the front gate as the rest of the group continued toward the stalls. I watched the two follow the men at a distance, speaking back and forth until I saw my father pull the reigns back stopping the horse in its tracks, his body stiffened as his head turned toward my window spotting me. I froze in fear knowing that my condition was now exposed.

I watched him dismount and drop the reigns. My brother also dismounted and followed him, speaking loudly but not loud enough for me to hear. I watched my father turn and push my brother forcefully, almost knocking him to the ground. Without taking his eyes from me, he moved toward the castle.

As soon as he disappeared through the front entrance, I sat on my bed and prepared for his fury.

The door flew open and my father's huge form filled the opening, his face flushed red and his huge hands were balled up in fists. He came to within inches of my face.

"When I did not heed your mother's warnings and indulged your whims, I did not realize the weight of my error. For that I will ask forgiveness but you who go against God will suffer the consequences and I rebuke the bastard you carry."

His words stung my face. He was tall and proud, and his frame could block out the sun. He had always had a gentle spot for his daughter, but at this moment he was on the battlefield and I was the enemy.

"He wants to marry me," I said softly.

"You have no idea what you have done." He backed up and unclenched his fists. His anger was melting into disappointment, which hurt so much worse than if he had just hit me. "You have betrayed our ancestors and all that we fought for. Every drop of Welsh blood was now spilled for naught. You are no daughter of Wales, and I will never bless a union that will destroy my country."

The tears I fought hard to hold back now flowed freely down both cheeks, further demonstrating my weakness, causing my father to shake his head in disgust as he turned and left my chamber pausing for one last message, "Today I leave without a daughter and I hope my heir will destroy those who come against these borders even if they are your sons."

My greatest fear was that he would be disappointed but thought he would see the benefits of the union. The child I carried was of his blood too. I was shocked that he so easily left my side completely. I was his only daughter. How could he so casually throw me away and now wish the death of my sons?

It was not my fault that Wales was in such a state. Our Welsh lands had endured Viking attacks for five generations and survived. The Norman threat could easily be distinguished if the Welsh could work together. Our defenses were weakened when my great grandfather, Rhodri the Great, decided to split Wales between his three sons and since have spent their resources against each other instead of the Norman invaders.

Was I not a vessel of the future? If I have a son, he could be the conduit of peace between nations. If I had a daughter, it would be of no consequence but could create another alliance. How could he not see the value of the situation? I needed Henry to speak with my father and assure him of the peace this would create.

Days, weeks, and months passed with no word from Henry. I was desperate as my belly grew, providing a constant reminder of my betrayal. I stayed out of my father's sight but would often take up a position outside his working chamber to listen for any news.

Even Gruffydd became distant as the pressure of the only child was thrust upon him. I followed my mother and brother one afternoon to my father's chamber but stayed hidden but close enough to hear their words.

"King William is dead," my father announced. I heard my mother gasp.

"How? "she asked.

"He was run down by his own horse," my father said.

"Is Prince Robert now the King of England?" Gruffydd asked.

"That should have been the rightful succession but William passed over his first-born and chose the third born, William Rufus is the new ruler of England."

"But the church—" my mother started.

"William is the new King of England. Robert is now the Duke of Normandy."

"What about Henry?" my mother and brother both asked at the same time.

"I don't know and don't care," my father said.

"William will be a horrible king," my mother said.

"I wonder if he will take a wife?" Gruffydd asked.

"He will have to marry but I pity the woman that has to share his bed," my mother said.

I couldn't hear another word. I had to speak with Henry as soon as possible. It was almost past the point where we could get married and have the child be declared legitimate. I could stay hidden in Wales until the child was a few months old before we declared its birth. There were very few who knew but it was becoming more obvious and impossible to hide even under the most generous gowns. If Henry did not secure his father's blessing, I fear all hope is lost.

When Henry finally arrived, I was thankful both my father and brother were hunting in the farthest part of the forest so that we could speak without interference, but as soon as I saw Henry's face, I knew there would be no peace. Henry's normally smiling face was slack and the glow in his cheeks had gone pale.

"I love you," I said in his ear, as I wrapped my arms around his middle and he put his face in my hair.

"It's not good, my love," he said.

"What's happened?"

"My father, William the Conqueror, had survived hundreds of battles and only suffered a few scars but it was his horse whose hoof found a mole hill that did him in. The horse fell and landed on top of him. By all accounts, he got up and remounted but his injuries were not obvious. His suffering continued until he was confined to his chamber bed. By the time I arrived, he had already dictated his last testament and was recorded by the Archbishop himself."

"I heard my father say that your brother, William, was named King."

"I don't know what his motivations were or if William had convinced him somehow to skip Robert but it is done. Robert has already opposed the action with the church but the Archbishop will not reverse my father's last wishes and William will wear the crown."

"What about our marriage?" I bowed my head, worried

for the answer.

"I did not have an opportunity to gain my father's blessing, but William had informed him of the child and in response left me no land and no title. I am now at my brother's mercy."

"How did he know about the child?"

"William pays well for information and although we have kept it close, the promise of silver is just too great," he said.

"But only people close to me have such information."

"Your belief in your people is admirable but also naïve," he said.

"So now what can we do?"

"I will have to convince my brother somehow the benefit to him in a union, but his nature will dictate the outcome. As King, he has control of whom I marry and when. I'm afraid he has my life in his hands."

"But what about the baby?" I touched my belly and felt a flutter. I reached out and put Henry's hand where the movement had happened. The child moved again causing Henry to smile widely.

"I will figure it out. I promise you," he said.

But Henry didn't figure it out and months later, I christened my son, Robert fitz Roy, at Saint David's without his father present. I named my brother, Gruffydd, as his godfather and holy protector and my mother as his godmother.

Robert was almost a month old when Henry was finally able to meet his child. He kissed my head before taking the tiny bundle from my arms. His face beamed with pride as he unwrapped his son to get a full view. Robert squirmed and cooed for his father. I saw a tear form in the corner of Henry's eye that he wiped away before it escaped.

"He is a fine boy, Nesta." Henry looked into my eyes with some concern and repeated. "A fine boy."

"He resembles his father, don't you think?"

"He does," he said, looking back to his son. He kissed him on the head before handing him back to me.

I sat on the edge of my bed, welcoming my son back into

my arms as my breast swelled, eager to relieve my son's hunger. I chose to feed him myself rather than rely on a wet nurse. I could not bear to be apart from him even for a few minutes.

"We have a problem," Henry said.

"I'm sure it isn't as grave as the look on your face," I said, looking down at our son in my arms. This small bundle that had erased all my worldly worries.

"The trouble between my brothers has escalated. Someone we thought was a trusted ally has turned traitor. He has warned William that Robert and I have been conspiring against him."

"What does that mean?"

"William knows that our child is a son and has refused to grant a marriage between us," Henry said as he sat next to me. He laid a hand on my knee, and I looked up and saw the woman that had been standing in the doorway behind Henry.

"Who is she?"

"William does not want there to be a legitimate heir. Even an illegitimate healthy boy is a threat, and I am afraid that he sees our son as that very threat."

"What are you trying to say, Henry?"

"Our child's life is in danger, at the very least he becomes a pawn in the hands of William."

"William will not get near my son. I promise you that," I said, pulling my son closer to my swollen breasts.

"I'm so sorry." Henry hung his head.

"Who is she?" I asked again, beginning to panic.

He ignored the question and continued a speech I could no longer hear. All I heard was "safe place... educate... far away..."

"We can keep him safe here. There are very few who know his lineage."

"You fool yourself, Nesta, this birth is well known, and there is no way for me to claim him unless there is a change to the crown," Henry said.

Henry stood in front of me and put his huge hands on my

face. "I promise you that this will pass, and that I will bring the country together so that you will again be united with your son. The love I have for you is real. I need you to trust me."

"You are not taking my son," I said firmly, and squeezed him too hard, causing him to cry. I rose from where I sat gently rocked him back and forth until he quieted, ignoring Henry and turning myself to face the wall, isolating my son and myself from the rest of the room.

Tears filled my eyes and rolled freely as I kissed his small cheek. This was not the life I had imagined. Everything was changing too fast. Henry stood behind me and put a heavy hand on my shoulder. I attempted to shake it off, but he moved to stand behind me.

"I beg you, don't do this!" I cried keeping my back to him, now helpless in matters of my own life. I whispered "I will not forsake you, my beautiful son. I will visit you in your dreams until the day we will reunite."

I turned back to face Henry and he reached under the bundle and gently lifted my son from my arms, leaving a cold empty void hanging from my heart. He turned and I followed until he handed the baby to the woman who had been quietly waiting. He turned back to face me, blocking my view.

"Nesta, I promise you."

"You are a traitor. I hate you." I pushed him with both my hands flat on his chest. Henry turned and walked out, hanging his head low as I followed close behind until we reached the courtyard. There was a large carriage where the woman was already settled, holding my child close.

I watched Henry kiss our son on top of his head before he mounted his horse. The carriage rolled away, surrounded by Henry's men. My eyes never left the carriage until there was complete silence. The world had stopped. I stood alone as the earth crumbled around me leaving me on a narrow plateau, too numb to feel the bite of the wind and too weak to call out.

CHAPTER 5

I thought I knew every tree, rock, and stream in these woods. I spent my childhood searching for magical creatures, climbing trees, and building forts along these paths, but today I found myself in an unfamiliar place, landmarks I did not recognize. I had run with no purpose other than to lose myself, taking unfamiliar turns and jumping over fallen trees. The blue sky disappeared, and the sun sank, turning orange and then red somewhere behind me. In the dark, the paths were now unrecognizable. The branches of the trees shielded the moonlight, and I tripped over an unseen stone.

I welcomed the skinned knee and the knot on my head, as they provided a distraction from the pain in my heart. I thought of the river and how easy it would be to fill my pockets with stones and jump in to escape the sadness if not for the promises I whispered to my son. I was so weary, and my heart so broken. My father's rejection was still raw, and my arms were empty, now that my baby had been taken away. My life had little meaning.

After several unsuccessful attempts to find my way out of the thick woods, I settled under the protective cover of a large weeping willow, whose branches heavy with new growth surrounded me like a curtain. I wrapped my cloak tightly around me and settled on the soft ground near the trunk. It wasn't long before my exhaustion took hold and the sound of night lulled me into a deep sleep.

I awoke to find two bright blue eyes staring curiously at me. I didn't startle, but simply sat up to face the girl sitting on the ground next to me. I wiped my eyes to make sure I wasn't dreaming, but she didn't disappear. She looked close to my age but with flaming red hair, full of curls, that was tangled with dried leaves and small twigs. I imagined a small mouse or two could easily live in the mess.

"Hello," the girl said with the thick Irish accent of a commoner. Her lips were naturally red, and I believed she never had to berry stain them.

"Hello," I said.

"You look too fine a lady to be bedding in the woods," she said.

I liked the singsong sound of her voice mixed with the accent. "I probably don't look much like a lady right now," I said, brushing leaves and twigs from my own hair.

"Would you have anything to eat?" she asked.

"I'm afraid I do not. It seems I lost my way after dark."

"You treat your life lightly, traveling in the wood with no escort."

"Same as you, I imagine," I said.

"I've escaped after a disagreement with my traveling companions. Neither of us will be safe if they come across us."

"How did you find me?" I asked.

"I heard you crying. At first, I thought it was a wounded animal, but as I approached, I saw just a girl. By the time I got near enough, the sobbing turned to snoring. I didn't want to wake you and start the sobbing again, so I just curled up over there for the night." She pointed to a flattened section of leaves a few feet from where I had been sleeping. "I figured two against one, better odds."

"Well, I thank you, that was very considerate," I said, and my stomach growled.

"What is your name?" I asked.

"Brigit," she said.

"My name is Nesta," I said. I stood and stretched, my body reminding me of my injuries of yesterday. I separated the curtain of branches and saw that I recognized the path.

I reached for the girl's hand and she eagerly reached back

out, allowing me to help her to her feet.

"Come," I said, pulling her with me through the branches.

We took the familiar path no longer blurred by tears, hand in hand.

"How did you come to these woods," I asked the girl covered in a layer of road dust.

"My journey began in Ireland more than a fortnight ago," she said, "The cruelty of a mother drove me from the shores of my homeland only to land me in the possession of men without my best interest in mind."

"Did they harm you?"

"They never got the chance. I shouldn't have trusted them, but I had only a few pennies to my name, so it was important to make allies on the ship as we crossed the Irish Sea. Most of the passengers were families and rejected my attempts at friendship but Lynal and his brother, Rollo took pity."

"Did it not work out?"

"While we were on the ship, things seemed to go smoothly enough. Sometimes their words were cruel, but at least I was fed. Rollo was the nicer of the two, but Lynal was in control of the decisions. Aside from their behavior, the two men looked so much alike that it took several days to figure out which was which."

"Were you not afraid that they would demand more?" I asked.

"That is why I escaped. As soon as we left the ship and were on the roads, Lynal decided my responsibilities included sharing a bed sack. When I rejected the idea, he became violent and beat me. He threatened to tie me to a tree and have his way forcibly. I had no choice but to sneak away in the middle of the night."

"That's awful," I said.

"Not too awful. It seems my fortune has changed."

"What do you mean?"

"I met a lady in the center of the wood. But I am sure you were not put here to wait for me, hidden under a tree. What troubles brought you into the middle of the forest?"

"I lost my child," I said hanging my head.

"The world is a cold place for the wee ones. Sometimes they are better in heaven sleeping with angels than to suffer here on earth."

"Oh, no. He is a healthy boy just over a month old. He was taken by his father under a vow of protection, but I am his mother and should have been allowed to go with him." As I spoke, I felt the pain fresh again.

"I, too, lost a child in such a way," Brigit said, causing me to freeze in my tracks. I turned to face her directly, and she reached to brush away a strand of hair that had come loose and hung in my face.

"Your child was taken from you too?" I asked.

"My mother sold my chastity to an important man in our town, and after a few times, my bleeding stopped, and my belly swelled. When the child was born, I felt like my life had a purpose, and the torments of my life seemed small. But as my own son reached a few months old, the man came with his wife claiming the boy as his property. Being so low born, I couldn't fight him. It seems the wife was barren, and this was the arrangement made with my mother. When she came home and found no child in my arms, she demanded the silver promised her for the child."

"That is awful," I said.

"I went to the man's home and he threw me out, warning me never to return. He did throw some pennies at me. I was careful picking them up and hiding them in the hem of my cloak. I didn't go home but paid the passage from Ros Ailithir, inland of County Cork, a place I will never see again."

"Our children are born in the same season then," I said, feeling the ache in my still swollen breasts.

"Yes, my lady. It seems so." She bent her head as a small breeze caused the fallen leaves to swirl around us. We continued our journey.

As we walked together silently side by side, I realized this girl was sent to me as a gift. She was unfortunate, mourning the loss of her child as I was, but her low status made her more vulnerable.

"Where are we going?" Brigit asked.

"Dinefwr," I said. "It's not too much farther."

"Is that your home?"

"It is. Would you like stay for a while?" I asked, looking her over. She looked to be a handsome girl, if the road grime was washed from her face. Taming the hair situation, however, might be a challenge. I doubted that a comb could accomplish such a feat, but I would try. I could help her turn an unfortunate situation into an opportunity.

"I have no other engagement," she said, smiling. "But what of the lady of the house? She is likely to reject me because of my appearance." She moved her hands from the top of her head to her face.

"She won't reject you, of that I am sure."

"How can you be so sure? Most houses are suspicious of strangers," she said.

"I am the lady," I said.

"What? "

"Actually, my mother is, but I will provide a proper gown and a quick brush through that hair, and she will be as impressed as I am." Brigit stopped and faced me. Smiling wide, she hugged me.

Although it was a bold move, I hugged her back. I was excited at the thought of having the company of someone my age who could talk about more than marriage and fashion. I was looking forward to more adventure stories from this strange exotic girl from across the Irish Sea.

"Were you not married to the father of your wee one?" she asked.

"It's complicated, as he was the son of a king. He is now a brother to the king, who has forbidden the marriage."

"A king!" she said in surprise.

"It would have been better if he had been a shopkeeper.

Without these complications, my child would still be in my arms."

"Even a shopkeeper has complications," she said. "There is hierarchy in every profession."

"I suppose so," I said.

"I told Henry we should run away and live anonymously, but he just laughed. I do know he owns the land in Pembroke, near my family, purchased with money his father left him." I wasn't sure I should share this with Brigit. The information only came to me when the Bishop shared it with my brother, who shared it with me.

Eventually, the walls of Dinefwr appeared on the horizon, and the familiar sounds of the Tywi River welcomed me home.

Dinefwr was an unassailable fortress as it was built on the top of a rock too steep on both the northern or southern approach and the River Tywi provided the protection of a thousand men. The journey was long, so it was a relief to see the guards riding toward us. Even the bare back of the mare was a relief to my tired legs.

We entered through the curtain wall, and my mother ran out to greet us with tears in her eyes. As soon as I dismounted, she threw her arms around me.

"Where have you been, child?" Her eyes were red and swollen, obviously she had been upset all night. "I sent men to find you!"

"I was lost," I said. I watched her face as her sorrow turned into anger.

"Impossible. You could find your way blindfolded in those woods," she said. "And who is this?" She pointed at Brigit, withholding as much disgust as she could to maintain a polite tone.

"Brigit is her name, Mother. She found me in the woods last night and kept me company." I didn't say more, as I didn't even know Brigit was there until I woke up.

"Where are you traveling from, child" she asked Brigit, examining the girl slowly from her curly red top to her feet covered with days of travel dust. So much for improving her appearance before presenting her to my mother.

"Ireland," Brigit said. She bowed her head slightly, keeping her blue eyes on my mother. "The County Cork to be specific, my lady."

"She has no place to go," I said in a pleading tone. I searched my mother's face for the slightest hint of compassion. My mother's face didn't change. Instead, her expression remained emotionless until she blinked several times ready to make her judgment.

"We can get you something to eat, and you may rest here tonight before you continue your journey," my mother said, conveying no sense of welcome.

"But Mother," I said softly, "she has no place to go. I was hoping she could stay here at the castle as one of my maids."

Even though we hadn't discussed this arrangement, Brigit quickly nodded her head in hopeful agreement.

My mother was already shaking her head in disapproval and motioned to her maid, Willa.

"Take her," my mother said, dismissing the two women by a wave of the back of her hand.

I watched Willa lead Brigit around the tower toward the kitchens. Before they disappeared, Brigit looked back toward me with wide eyes and a hopeful look on her face. I smiled reassuringly but knew my mother would be hard to convince.

"What do you know of this girl?" My mother instinctively moved to put her body in between me and the path the two women had just taken.

"I know she needs our help," I said.

"I could walk the village and point to many people who could use our help," she said.

"I can't help but believe destiny had a hand in this meeting. She has escaped the vilest circumstances. For us to find each other in the middle of the forest is surely divine intervention. She could have easily robbed me, but she only offered kindness. Does that not show integrity?"

"A thief is not a thief until there is something to steal. What of value did you carry into the woods? The integrity you speak of does not belong to those who live in dire circumstances, one whose future is so uncertain that they are driven by the need to survive, and whose instinct drives their every decision. You are a fool to believe this girl will never bond with you and in time will surely betray your trust. No matter what kindness you offer, her actions will only be in her own interest. I am not laying blame to her future actions if not for the circumstances in what she was born into."

"She needs me," I said, unconvinced.

"No, my dear, I fear it is you who think you need her." My mother shook her head in defeat.

"What if I promise not to fully trust her and keep a watchful eye toward her?" I put both hands together as if I was praying.

"I will allow this as a distraction to your sorrow, but not without great hesitation. It is obvious a lesson you must learn on your own. I pray the heartache will not be of any consequence."

I wrapped my arms around my beautiful mother and hugged her tightly. She held me there longer than comfortable as if she was holding on to me for the last time. Finally, breaking apart, I weaved my arm in hers with new lightness in my steps as we walked arm in arm to the kitchen. Willa was busy moving around the kitchen space until she settled at the bread table expertly working the dough with a punch and a twist. Brigit sat at one end of the long wooden table shoveling spoon after spoon into her mouth until the large bowl of boiled barley covered in my mother's own honey had disappeared.

As soon as I sat next to her, a matching bowl appeared in front of me. I was so hungry I didn't even take time to acknowledge Willa's hand that placed it there. Brigit, still hungry, helped herself to another bowl from the kettle near the stove. Willa continued pushing on her ball of dough but keeping an eye on the girl. My mother stood for a moment but shook her head slowly before disappearing out the back door. Later, I would find her in the garden pulling the weeds that threatened the orderly rows of the delicate new sprouts that had appeared like magic overnight.

CHAPTER 6

After a long soak in a hot bath and plenty of oil applied to her hair, Brigit looked like a different girl. Her skin was red from the scrubbing it took to remove the grime, but she was gorgeous. Her red hair had been tamed and plaited against her head.

Willa reluctantly provided her with a clean white shift that she was wearing when I arrived with a few of my old gowns. I handed her a soft blue one that perfectly matched her eyes. As she slipped the gown over her head and adjusted the laces, she transformed from a street urchin to a lovely girl. No one would believe she wasn't a lady.

"You look wonderful," I said.

"I feel like my skin is burning off," she said, as she turned and watched the gown move with her.

I handed her a pair of light tan slippers that were a bit too small and watched her struggle to get them on. I finished lacing the bodice from the back, forcing her breasts to swell in the front. She was well-endowed in all the right places.

If only I could figure out how Brigit's birth was tied to a royal or a landowner, even as an indiscretion, I knew my mother would permit her to serve as a housemaid. I would soon enlist the services of Anthony, one of the bishops of Irish descent at Saint David's. He could surely trace a lineage from Ireland. In the meantime, I would teach her to look and act like a lady.

I took Brigit by the hand, proud to be a part of her transformation. I wanted to show her through the castle.

We entered the kitchen where my mother was giving final instructions for the evening meal.

"Mother," I said, but she didn't even bother to look up.

"Nesta, please. Your father is returning this evening with a full contingent. Let's add another shoulder of pork and apricot cakes." Obviously, she was no longer speaking to me, so I simply pulled Brigit out the back door.

As soon as we reached the garden gate, Gruffydd appeared almost out of nowhere causing us to jump.

"I hate when you do that, Gruffydd," I said.

"My only sin is a light step, while you walk with your head in the clouds," he said smiling.

"And who is this lovely lady?" he asked.

"Gruffydd, may I present Brigit, and Brigit, may I present my brother, Gruffydd."

"My pleasure," she said, smoothly with a light curtsy, giving me renewed hope for a complete transformation.

"At your service." My brother bowed slightly and stood awkwardly in front of us as if he had never seen a pretty girl before.

"When did you get home?" I asked my brother.

"Late, while you were gone. Mother was crazy with worry. Where were you?"

Gruffydd said but was curiously distracted by Brigit, which was surprising, because his interests were mainly crossbows and horses.

"What is wrong with you?" I asked him, hoping to shake him from his stare.

Gruffydd shook his head like he was waking from a trance. Then a huge smile appeared on his face. "I got a falcon."

"A falcon?"

"Yes. Look." He held out his arm to show us a thick leather sleeve that covered his forearm. Three leather straps with engraved silver buckles held it in place. He also wore a matching leather glove.

"Where did you get a falcon?" I asked.

"Father brought it from the North. It is mostly trained."

"Where is father?" I asked, "and where is the falcon?"

"Father is in the wood, hunting and the falcon is in his

pen."

"So where are you going?" I asked.

"I need to get ready for the King."

"William is coming here?" I asked excitedly. "Will Henry be with him?"

"I don't know," my brother said, as if annoyed by my question. He still had not forgiven my indiscretion.

"Go play with your falcon," I said, dismissing him. He left, but not before taking another long look at Brigit.

"Your brother is very handsome, and tall." Brigit raised one eyebrow as she carefully watched him walk away.

"He is betrothed to Gwenllian of Gwynedd," I said quickly, having noticed her interest.

"Is she beautiful?" Brigit asked.

"I believe so. I have heard songs written of both her beauty and bravery," I said. "But beauty aside, we have no say in who we marry. Unfortunately, politics dictate our future. I was to be wed to Owain of Powys, which, along with Gruffydd's marriage, would have aligned all three Welsh countries. My father is a strategic man and planned carefully, but Owain has been banned from this country. Now, I would like to marry Henry."

"Will your father not allow it?" she asked.

"Hopefully that is the reason King William is here, to arrange my marriage to Henry."

"How do you know your father will agree?"

"I don't know what he will say. Ever since he found out about the child, he hasn't spoken a word to me. My heart is in a thousand pieces over the shame and disappointment I caused my father, but my love for Henry has taken over my soul. Henry promised to create a treaty to ensure the safety of Welsh lands, hoping to gain my father's blessing."

"You are such a fortunate girl, Nesta," said Brigit, smiling at me.

"We are both fortunate, and I'm glad I met you," I said.

I continued to show Brigit the castle, including the vast gardens surrounding it. This was where my mother spent her time, pruning each plant as if it were the only one of its kind. Her worst complaints described the battles against thistles that somehow invaded the roses despite her extensive efforts to stop their advances. Our inventory of the different colors and fragrances was interrupted by the familiar thunder of war-horses riding in pairs across the wooden drawbridge.

My heart began to race when I saw the King's colors. I took Brigit's hand and led her to the courtyard in front of the stable where the men would dismount. My mother had also taken her place of greeting when they reached us.

Several of the knights tipped their heads in greeting as they passed, heading to where the stable boys waited to tend the horses.

"This is so exciting," Brigit said, pinching my arm so hard that it stung. Before I could complain, I saw Henry's beautiful face surrounded by dark hair that he let grow a few inches past his shoulders since the last time I had seen him. He smiled and nodded at me.

My heart was unsettled as I watched the men dismount and release their heavy cloaks and metal to the waiting arms of the squires. Henry's tunic was deep blue, heavy with gold brocade just like the first time I saw him. My mother stood tall next to Henry, and I admired her. I had never really noticed her strength.

"Welcome, Prince Henry." My mother bowed her head slightly.

"If it's not the fairest Queen in all the land, and her lovely young daughter," Henry said, kissing each of our right hands and winking at me. He noticed the young ginger standing near me and said, "And who is the new addition?"

"May I present my friend, Brigit," I said, feeling a twinge of jealousy as he looked her up and down, as every other man had done since I brought her home. My mother also noticed his attention and shook her head in disapproval.

"I'm afraid Rhys has not returned from his morning hunt," my mother said, "but the chamber has been prepared for your meeting." I knew she was attempting to distract him. She still held great resentment for the heartache he had caused our family. The birth of our child was known only to the castle household and few others. And while they were all sworn to secrecy, they knew of Henry's attentions toward me.

I noticed Henry's continued appraisal of Brigit, but his focus was soon back entirely upon me. He looked into my eyes and the rest of the world became less important. I longed for his touch and the way he pushed the stray curls behind my ears before he kissed me.

"Let us get you and your men settled." My mother spoke loudly, with a touch of irritation in her voice, hoping to distract the young prince from his obvious attention to her daughter's body. He smiled, turned to my mother, and humbly bowed, following her to the meeting chamber.

"We were expecting the King," I heard her say as I trailed behind.

"Unfortunately, he was delayed in important negotiations. He sent his full authority with me," Henry said.

"Brigit," my mother said without looking directly at her, "make arrangements for food and drink for Henry and his men."

Brigit's eyes got wide and her jaw clenched, but she turned toward the kitchen. My mother had put her in her place. It was obvious she was not going to accept her as my companion but treating her simply as another servant in our household.

I was worried that Brigit would take offense, then surprised as she moved past Henry's men, smiling and batting her eyes at Gowri Golden Hair. He nodded and winked in return. My mother also caught the gesture. She rolled her eyes and shook her head as she excused herself and walked toward the kitchen behind Brigit.

Henry took this opportunity to lead me by the arm to an alcove away from the direct view of others. When we stood face to face, his pleasant look turned to one of anguish.

"Will William allow our union?" I asked.

"I don't know. His mind is devious, and he will be looking

for alliances to create strategic unions. The only way I can influence his decision is to show a benefit for him and I am struggling with the task."

"A Welsh alliance with my father, the most powerful Welshman in the land, would certainly be viewed as a profitable union. The Welsh will surely reject William, and it will be my father who can keep the peace."

"I agree, but William is unpredictable. I don't trust him, and neither should your father. Negotiation on my brother's behalf is not my real purpose here."

"Then what is your purpose?"

"Gowri Golden Hair believes one of the men is passing information to William for reward. Robert and I have a plan that may be treasonous on the surface, but the unrest created with William on the throne is a danger to all of us," Henry said.

"What does that have to do with my father?"

Instead of answering, he pointed to the gates where my father and his men were coming across the bridge. The large horses were trotting at a slow pace through the gates leading a mule-led cart heavy with venison, guarded by the untethered staghounds. When they reached the stables, a young attendant accepted the reins from my father as he smoothly dismounted from the large, dapple-gray hunting stallion. Another boy gathered the staghounds and took them back to the hound pens for their reward. As they approached the fenced area, I could hear a fresh litter making a fuss at their parent's return.

"You must go," Henry said. "I don't want to further inflame your father."

He kissed me hard and then walked me to the door. I moved out of sight but didn't go far. I waited for my father and his men to arrive at the meeting chamber. I watched as Henry transformed into the regal representative of the King, and the two most important men in my life addressed each other as equals in a complicated world.

The thick door was closed, so even with my ear close, I could not make out their words. Soon, Brigit arrived with two jugs of ale for the men. She saw me and smiled conspiratorially. I moved back out of sight. She knocked lightly and opened the door. After delivering the ale, she came back out and pushed the door almost closed, leaving a small gap to peer through. When the men continued their conversation, she motioned me over and we stood together and listened.

"Those are things to discuss later, but officially, I am here to bring news of unrest in Breckon and request Welsh forces to support the West."

"Why would William trust you as a messenger?" my father asked.

"He could have sent his seal, but my intentions are well known by my brother."

"I can handle Breckon and I will accept the King's request, with the condition that reduced rents will fund this support," my father said. "But Wales is my first priority, and I will not support an uprising against an English king if it weakens my country."

"My brother has also sent enough silver to enlist Madog's forces to aid in the endeavor," Henry told my father.

"Madog will likely make things worse," my father said.

"It is his request," Henry said. "You may still have reduced rents, and an extra donation to Saint David's."

There was silence, and the creaking chairs warned Brigit and me to move away from the door. We quietly moved along the hall, down the stairs past the kitchen, and through the garden door where we found a bench on which to sit.

"What was that all about?" she asked.

"I don't know, but it doesn't sound good."

After the meal, we followed the men to the courtyard, staying at a distance. When Henry and his men reached the front courtyard, the stable boys had their horses ready. I watched my father reach out to Henry for a vigorous handshake. My father saw me standing away but didn't turn or acknowledge me. When he was out of sight, Henry came to face me.

"When will I see you again, my love?" I asked Henry.

"I promise it won't be long," he said, effortlessly mounting and pulling the reins to turn the horse.

"How is our son?" I asked, "Have you seen him?"

"Robert is fine. His foster parents are well established, and he is flourishing, I assure you, but more importantly, he is safe."

"I miss him so much," I said.

"He is safe." He reached down from his horse and touched the top of my head.

I walked back and stood next to Brigit and watched Gowri Golden Hair mount his horse. He winked at Brigit and blew her a kiss from the palm of his hand. I looked at her in shock.

"How dare that man," I said, "he doesn't even know you."

"Oh, he does know me, every bit of me," she said. She turned and walked away, leaving me standing with my mouth open, watching Henry leave me once again.

CHAPTER 7

My father and brother took a small contingent north to the land of Gwynedd to gather support for the battle at Breckon with the King's silver. The lands of Gwynedd were known for experienced Welshmen who were more than willing to raise their swords for a bag of silver no matter if the opponent was of their own blood.

In the small village of Bangor, they found Madog, the most notorious Welsh warrior for hire. My father was familiar with Madog's tactics as he had opposed him on the battlefield more than once. As they arrived through the gates, it looked more like an armor-clad organized band of thieves than a professional military force.

My mother and I stood in our places of greeting as the men arrived behind my father.

"You must stay clear of these men," my mother said still facing forward.

"I plan to," I said.

"These are cruel and vicious men who use war as justification to rape and pillage. They take as much pleasure in leaving a path of destruction as much as they count on the silver in their pockets. Do not trust them, they have no loyalty."

I stood silent until I saw Madog ride past. I knew right away who he was from a bard's song. He was a head shorter in height and twice as wide as most Welshmen. He had a flattened nose, wide lips, and wisps of black hair growing only around his ears. The lyrics of the song say he was the son of a Knocker who had raped his mother during the darkest night of the winter solstice.

He truly was repulsive to look at with scars on both his cheeks and a blinded eye he didn't bother covering. Gruffydd told me the damage to his face was not born in battle but the result of forcibly sticking his prick into a whore's mouth, and her twin sister attacked him with his own blade.

"Send Brigit to deliver the baskets," my mother said, "and you stay out of sight. This mess will clear in a few days."

But my curiosity and Brigit's encouragement brought me to the door of the hut where Madog and his men had set up as their lodging quarters. This was the largest hut inside the castle walls normally used for storing winter wheat. I knocked on the wooden door even though it stood wide open.

"Come," said a voice inside.

I hesitated long enough that Brigit pushed me from behind, forcing me past the threshold.

"We have brought fresh fruit for you and your men," Brigit said as she moved past me confidently. I stood frozen, looking around as if I had never been in this hut before. I was used to seeing the walls lined with barrels of wine and ale but now the furthest wall was stacked with various weapons and tackle. In the center of the room, a peat fire smoldered beneath a large round pot hanging from a metal frame. The insufficient opening cut into the thatched roof on one side, caused the smoke from the fire to collect at the ceiling above our heads.

"Come, child," Madog motioned to me with a bent finger.

"We brought bread and fruit from the kitchen," I said repeating what Brigit had already announced.

"Leave it." He pointed to the floor next to the steaming pot hanging over a fire in the middle of the hut. I entered and set it down quickly. I could feel greedy eyes following my every move, but it was Brigit that attracted the most attention. As she leaned over to deliver her basket, one of the men reached out and pulled her into his lap. I gasped, but she was giggling. I put the basket down and hurried out, standing outside the door, hoping Brigit would soon follow.

I heard Madog say, "Let her go," and Brigit came out a few

seconds later.

"What a rowdy bunch they are," she said, still smiling.

The next few days were filled with commotion as the men readied for battle. Carts full of weapons and supplies arrived daily as meetings over unrolled maps took place on any flat surface available. This seemed to be a serious battle which made my stomach turn as I saw my father's serious face bent over one of the larger maps. I had never experienced this much preparation for battle before. I worried for my father, but my mother remained calm.

The mild weather seemed to vanish overnight. The troops assembled, some on great warhorses, some on foot all carrying longbows. The sky turned dark as clouds gathered overhead threatening a torrential rain. I began to feel even more nervous as I stood next to my mother who finally showed a bit of distress, twisting her fingers and shifting from one foot to the other. I reached for her hand and held it tightly.

The War bell rang just as the first drops of rain hit the earth and the front gates opened releasing the forces led by my father with Madog at his side. The rebels would have no chance against such a powerful force. Perhaps it was the extreme preparations that felt different from the many times we watched my father leave these gates to march against some enemy.

For years, we had enjoyed peace with the Normans and our Welsh neighbors, so there was little need for manning battlements, so we were left with just a few guards. It was a peace we had come to rely on.

That delicate peace was the reason my father thought enlisting Madog's participation was like *putting a lion in a rabbit's den*. He believed the new king was just eager to show his teeth, but he agreed reluctantly.

Days passed with no reports increasing the tension among us left behind. My mother stayed closed up in her chamber or busy in her garden. On the third day with no news, it was the arrival of Gruffydd and two of my father's best men that brought my mother and I rushing to the courtyard. Gruffydd's face was white with panic and his head heavy. He had blood stains on his tunic.

"What happened?" asked my mother, her voice shaking.

Gruffydd got off his horse and ran to her, putting both arms around her, pulling her to his chest, "I'm so sorry," he said.

"Where is he?" she asked my brother, tears already falling.

I could feel hot tears on my own cheeks as I watched my brother's tortured face.

"He's dead," Gruffydd said, hanging his head as my mother pushed away to look him in the eye.

"What happened?"

"When our troops reached Breckon, we found the rebels were not a military force but a simple group of farmers. They had banded together to protest the construction of a Norman castle being built on their land for Bernard of Neufmarche, whom William has granted lordship over the entire area. The farmers were easily dispersed, and only a few armed guards were required to maintain the peace."

Gruffydd looked exhausted, with tears falling from his own eyes. He choked and couldn't continue. My mother turned to Gowin. He came to stand with Gruffydd and placed a strong arm around him.

"Madog and his gang of bandits were not satisfied with easy peace and a full purse. They left Breckon looking for another target. King Rhys remained with a small contingent to ensure the dispute was settled. He approached Bernard with a proposal to compensate the displaced farmers with additional lands on which they could produce enough to enjoy a profit. Bernard would not negotiate, even when Rhys showed that it was in his best interest. When we went back to the farmers with the news, they attacked again but had no chance against Bernard's forces. Rhys was trapped between the two sides and was killed by Bernard himself."

"I fear it was orchestrated somehow," Hait spoke up.

As recognition dawned on my mother's face, she said, "We have to get you out of here, now," looking directly at Gruffydd.

"I agree," Gowin said. "Get back on that horse."

"But why?" My brother looked around, concerned.

"You are the only heir, the last Prince of Wales," Hait said, also mounting his horse.

"No, you stay with the Queen," Gowin told Hait. "I will get him to the ship."

"Go!" my mother ordered. I stood in shock watching my brother ride out of sight.

"Where will he go?" I asked her.

"Ireland," she said. "We established this contingency when he was born. We also must leave as soon as possible. We are no longer safe here."

"If Breckon was indeed a trap, as I believe it was, the new king is a threat," Hait said. "He will build alliances by promising Welsh lands to gain Norman supporters."

"We had a fragile relationship with King William I, and I feel that William II will not honor his father's promises, especially with your father gone. Without a Welsh King, Deheubarth belongs to William, and so do we," my mother said.

We spent all afternoon and evening getting ready to leave. I packed only essentials as we would only have one small cart for our belongings. I looked at the empty cradle near the end of my bed, thankful my son was safe but feeling the familiar ache in my heart. The exhaustion of the day finally overcame me, and I fell asleep, fully dressed, imagining my small son in a warm bed far away.

Loud voices and hounds barking soon woke me and an orange glow drew me to the window where I could see flames coming from several storage huts. The stables were fully engulfed, and the horses and dogs were loose and running frantically. The servants, arms full, attempted to save what they could and were fleeing through the front gate.

Morning hadn't fully broken, but I could see a full contingent of troops, right outside the castle gates, flying the familiar blue and gold standard of King William. Relief washed over me, cooling my panic, as I believed those colors represented Henry and his men here to save us.

I found my cloak and wrapped myself in it. I needed to find my mother and Brigit. I tripped over the cradle that I had moved. I felt the pain in my toe and my heart for just a few seconds before panic again took over.

I ran though the kitchen and out the side door to see what was happening. A large guard dressed in gray and black almost invisible in the pre-dawn, grabbed me by my hair and stopped me mid-stride. I yelped with pain as he pulled me off my feet. A few seconds later, the guard let go of my hair, dropped to his knees and fell face first into the dirt. Brigit stood over him with a large cast iron pot.

"We have to get out of here," I told her.

"I figured," she said, setting down the pan and grabbing my hand.

We moved quietly in the shadows until we reached the stables, but the horses that hadn't escaped were corralled and heavily guarded. We would have to escape through the forest on foot and come outside the wall to where Henry's men were waiting. I couldn't understand why they weren't helping.

As we rounded the corner of the stable, a huge knight appeared, blocking our escape. My panic weakened my legs, and I slumped to the ground. Brigit pulled at me to stand up. She was busy looking for an escape, while I was giving in to the belief that we would die here today. The large man now moved between the two of us, easily lifting me to my feet. His voice was deep, but he spoke with a calm, concerned tone.

"Come with me now," he said, directly to me while ignoring Brigit.

Brigit, realizing that this man was determined to leave her behind, picked up my cloak and carefully wrapped it around my shoulders.

"Not without me," she said.

"I have no desire to go with you anywhere," I said.

"There is little time to escape, my Lady," he said to me. "And I will not be slowed down by a kitchen wench," he said looking at Brigit who stood with hands on her hips.

"She is coming with me. If you want me to go with you as a prisoner or as a willing captive, you must also take the girl," I said.

"This girl is not my charge," he said shaking his head, "but if it will lead to your cooperation, I shall accept your terms. However, I will only guarantee your safety. She will serve as her own guardian."

"Don't you worry," Brigit said, "I can take care of myself."

"And I will keep my helmet safely on my head," he said. He whistled a long flat tone, signaling a comrade with two large and fully armored horses. He lifted me easily onto the black stallion and took his position behind me.

"Take the girl," he ordered the other man before he kicked the horse firmly and we rode into the woods away from the burning chaos.

"What about my mother?" I asked him. He kept silent.

When we had gone a safe distance into the woods, my protector stopped his horse and pulled off his helmet so I could see his face. It was Hait, my father's guard. I hadn't recognized him or his voice in all the confusion. His eyes were light brown with flecks of gold, and his dark hair was plastered to his head with perspiration. He wiped his face with a scarf he untied from his reins. "I do not know your mother's fate, but she is likely safe," he said. "She is no stranger to peril and will have found safety."

"Are you a spy?" I wanted to know his part in this upheaval.

"It's complicated," he said.

"But you helped my brother escape."

"You must never repeat that. Ever!"

"I don't understand. Are you not my father's guard?"

"It is Henry that sent me as your protector," he said. He looked kind, and I believed his intentions were genuine. "King William II has made me Sheriff of Pembroke as a reward."

"So, are you loyal to the new King and not my father?" I asked.

"Loyalty can be complicated. I choose mine with my heart, not my heritage. At this moment, I am in your service, and I am to deliver you to His Majesty," he said.

"Where is Henry?" I asked.

"I don't know," he said, pulling his helmet back over his head and his reins in the opposite direction from England.

"Where are we going?" I asked.

"We have to stop at Saint David's. Seems there was a skirmish while we were distracted," he said. I settled back against Hait, convinced by now that he was not my captor but my savior. I would not forget this day, being led away from Dinefwr castle. But somehow it was a relief. I was leaving the past behind to find a future that would likely include Henry.

CHAPTER 8

The day broke while we were deep in the woods. Traveling the road to Saint David's gave me some sense of normality and when I closed my eyes, I could hear the familiar sounds of the birds as they woke, and I could even smell the color of the trees. But the tranquility of the journey ended as soon as we emerged from the woods and saw the first of our tenant's farm destroyed. The crops had been burned to the roots and what was left of the fence posts lay on their sides. A heavily loaded cart came out a side path when they realized we were no danger. It was a farmer and his wife pushing the cart.

"Where are you heading, my friend?" Hait asked.

"Dinefwr, sir," the man answered.

"Dinefwr is burned and King Rhys is dead, I am afraid."

"We have nothing left and if we don't find a village, we will starve."

"Who did this?"

"It was a band of wild men robbing and burning the crops. They could have been Danes but spoke the northern language. Some say it was a Welshman leading the raids. Some have even lost their wives and daughters. They slaughtered our only cow."

"Head to the Tywi River and find Alfur, the boatman. You will find shelter for the night. Tell him Hait has sent you."

"Bless you, sir," the man said bowing his head and moved past.

"Who are these men who are terrorizing our country?" I asked, not expecting Hait to answer.

"It is Madog for sure. I vow today that the men who did this will pay," he said. "This destruction was not sanctioned by the King. He will have their heads if my sword doesn't find them first. I'm afraid this country will be torn apart now that your father is dead."

I felt deflated by those words. My father was dead, and our people were suffering without their King. We passed several more farms that had suffered destruction.

"Who will save our land?" I asked.

"King William will fill the void with a Norman Lord," he said.

"Won't the locals stand against the Normans like they did at Breckon?"

"You are safe, and your brother is safe. The future of this land is in now in your hands. Record this day and vow your protection when you are able."

"I don't understand."

"You will come to understand in time. For now, hold close your thoughts, do not expose your weaknesses and be wary of even your closest allies, for you will find no loyalties among them."

We rode in silence until finally Saint David's came into sight. I could always find comfort within its walls. Hait dismounted and helped me down, and I hurried to the rectory where I found Archbishop Rhygyfarch, who was inconsolable.

"They took everything, it's all gone," he said, "there was nothing we could do."

"Who is responsible?" I asked him.

"Madog," he answered. "I told him King Rhys will have his head on a pike for this. He just laughed and said the King is dead."

"That's impossible. How could he have known my father had died, unless—" I couldn't say it. Madog knew my father would not be able to make him pay for these actions. It was no accident that he was left in Breckon to die.

"Henry was the one who convinced my father to ride to Breckon with Madog," I whispered to Hait, "he must have known about the plot."

Hait shook his head to quiet me.

"Where is your brother?" Rhygyfarch asked worriedly.

"Hopefully he is safe in the Irish Sea," I said, "he escaped when we heard of my father's death. They burned us down. Hait saved me.

"Thank God," Rhygyfarch crossed himself. "There is hope, child."

I looked around at the church, everything of value was gone or destroyed. I barely recognized the space. I found no peace here.

"My Wales is gone," I whispered.

The Archbishop heard my words and placed a hand on my shoulder. "Wales is in here," he said, pointing to my heart. "You must trust God's plan, even in times like these." He wiped a tear from his own cheek before he wiped away mine.

"There is no God," I said. "My father dedicated his life to this country. How could Madog act so violently against his own people?"

"Madog is a wolf in Welsh clothing. He has no loyalty except to his purse. Hope is not lost. There is a legal heir and let us pray he stays safe. There are plenty of Welsh allies in Ireland who will make sure Gruffydd is ready for the future."

"What will become of you?" I asked. "You are Welsh."

"I am sure William will not replace me until peace is established in the region. He needs my influence with the people. I just don't know how to rebuild the stability Saint David represents. We have no relief for the villagers who have lost everything."

"We will take a message to the King and I am sure he will send relief, but we need to go," Hait said, as he came up behind me.

"I'm so sorry," Rhygyfarch said as he kissed the top of my head. "God be with you, child."

My heart was heavy as we rode away from the cold stone building that had lost its light. It was just then I saw the same Italian jeweled cross that Henry and I had stood in front of when we first met at Saint David's. Like Henry said, the thieves hadn't recognized its value because the jewels were buried deep within its construction with just a small bit of its glory peeking to the surface. The church's most valuable artifact still stood in plain sight.

"Where are you taking me?" I asked Hait, now trying to focus on my future.

"You are now the ward of King William Rufus and have his protection. I assure you, Princess, that you are safe under my care."

"Why would the King have me as a ward?" I asked, not really expecting an answer.

"I am not privy to the thoughts of the new King, but I would guess it is politically motivated. You are beloved by your people and the consort of his younger brother, Prince Henry. Rumors have surfaced that Prince Robert is not satisfied to be Duke of Normandy, and as the eldest son of William I, believes he is the rightful King of England. With these forces at play, you will ensure Henry's loyalty remain steady and not find an alliance with his brother Robert," Hait said, surprisingly open with his opinions.

"I see," I said softly, realizing my fate. I was a captive of King William Rufus, and my father Rhys ap Tewdor, King of South Wales, was dead. My brother, Gruffydd, would be living in exile in Ireland, and my family's land was now occupied by Normans.

"I wish my mother was here. I need her comfort."

"I am sorry, I wish I could provide that comfort," he said not looking back at me.

"Is the King responsible for the raid on Dinefwr?"

Hait stayed silent.

"The King sent my father to Breckon. He insisted he hire Madog. My father knew it was a bad idea. William is the reason my father is dead."

Hait pulled back on the reins so hard, the horse pulled to the side and I almost fell if Hait's arm hadn't pulled me back. I felt dizzy but gained my composure and once again sat tall.

"You are too free with your speech, my Lady. You are a ward of the King and you should not forget who your benefactor is. These words you say are treason and this King finds joy in torture. I promise to be your protector, but I am powerless if you expose yourself so readily." Hait jumped from the horse and took the reins in his hands. He motioned to the other horseman who had stayed behind.

The poor man's face was twisted as they came up next to us.

"I can't sit on this beast any longer. Can we take a break?" Brigit said.

"We will take shelter at Pembroke," Hait said.

"Thank God," the other man said also dismounting and walking next to Hait.

"Will it be safe?" Brigit asked.

"A lot safer than riding any further with me," he said.

"I don't know what that means, you fool," she said, "but it's your safety that should be more of a concern."

"Brigit, please be silent with complaints, these men have delivered us to safety," I said.

"We are about to arrive at Pembroke where we will stay the night. Gerald of Windsor protects the castle with a full contingent," Hait said.

I could hardly keep my eyes open, and several times almost slipped from my seat on the horse as the steady clop of the hooves put me in a trance.

When we finally made it to the gates, they opened almost silently, almost as if it was a dream, but the men at arms strategically placed around the battlements were very real. They wore full gear including full faced helmets as if they were expecting to be attacked. But the sheer number provided a strong sense of security. These were unfamiliar men, not the guards who protected these walls for my father.

Gerald, the new Castilian met us at the gate on his own stallion. He easily dismounted as did the two men-at-arms that accompanied him.

"Welcome, Sheriff," Gerald said with a slight bow.

"May I present Nesta, daughter of Rhys, Princess of Deheubarth," Hait said as he held his hand to help me off the horse.

"Welcome to Pembroke," he said, not looking at me directly.

"Thank you," I said, "and may I present Brigit, my companion."

Gerald looked toward Brigit but ignored her and instead, turned to lead us inside the castle walls. Hait took my arm and led me past small wooden huts with smoke rising from small holes cut into the thatched roofs. Larger huts had stone hearths with tall chimneys blowing the gray smoke into the darkening sky. These men were well established and here to stay.

As we entered the familiar hall, a large woman was ready to greet us.

"Please follow Maud who will take you to your chamber and wash up. The evening meal will be ready when you are," Gerald said.

"We thank you for your hospitality, my Lord," I said with some resentment, since these lands belonged to my people.

"It's been a long day," Hait said.

"Let's get you some dinner and some fresh clothes," Maud said. I looked back at Hait, who nodded his assent. I was exhausted and after a hot bath, just couldn't keep my eyes open.

I didn't make it to the meal and awoke the next morning forgetting where I was. Brigit was asleep next to me, snoring loudly.

"Brigit, wake up." I shook her softly, but she just rolled over and pulled the furs over her head.

I found a fresh shift and a light purple gown that was set out for me and slipped it on. I made my way to the kitchen in search of something to settle my rumbling stomach. I couldn't remember the last time I ate.

The kitchen was busy with morning preparations to break the fast. I sat at one of the benches at the long wooden table as I had as a child at this very table. Pembroke had been our home before Dinefwr was constructed. The smell of freshly baked bread filled my nostrils until someone grabbed me from behind, but when I turned, all I saw were two large breasts that were pressed into my face, making it hard for me to breathe at all. Finally, the owner of the breasts was revealed as she let me loose enough to stand. It was Willa, my mother's most loyal maid.

"My beautiful girl," she said with tears in her eyes.

"Oh Willa, you escaped. Have you seen my mother?" I hugged her tight.

"No dear, I heard about the raid from several of the staff who escaped. My daughter who works here has been assigned to her bed until the birth of the babies, so I have been here."

"Babies?"

"Yes, there are two and she is as big as a boat. Your mother released me to be with my daughter and I have been helping with the baking until she is back on her feet."

"Then I am fortunate if there are cinnamon circles in that oven," I said.

Willa moved to a side table and produced a full plate of cinnamon circles fresh from the oven. I had already eaten one before she set the butter beside me. I ate another roll and soon a plate of assorted meats and cheeses was set in front of me which I began to devour.

I wasn't very lady-like as I stuffed the alder-smoked ham and fresh goat cheese into my mouth when I noticed Gerald standing in the door that led out to the side garden. He was smiling as he watched me but still didn't look me directly in the eye.

"Good morning, Princess," he said.

"Good morning, Gerald," I said as I stood and bowed slightly in his direction.

"Please finish," he said motioning to me.

"I think I have had enough," I said pushing the plate aside.

"Then please," he said holding his hand to me.

I wiped my mouth with the cloth Willa had handed me and followed Gerald to the garden.

"Please," Gerald said motioning to the bench set in the center of the herbs.

The combined smells of new onion and fresh basil teased me as I wasn't completely full and wished I had one more of Willa's rolls.

"I'm sorry to hear of your father's death," he said.

I stayed silent, looking down at the sprigs of parsley at my feet.

"I served with him many times," he said.

"Do you know where my mother is?" I asked him, looking into his eyes as his finally met my own.

"I am afraid I do not," he said. He had light brown eyes with what looked like dark brown bursts from the center. They were quite unusual, and it was hard to look away. He lowered his eyes to my stare. His face was plain but interesting, especially the wide clef in his chin. My mother would have said this was a kiss from an angel, but I imagined he may have fell on an axe.

"I believe my mother may come here," I said.

"I promise my protection if she seeks refuge within these walls," he said again looking into my eyes.

Hait appeared from around the corner in his full riding gear. "We must go, Nesta. It's a full day's ride to our next stop."

I stood and followed him to the front of the castle where the horses were already loaded including Brigit, looking quite unhappy wrapped in an old shawl. It looked like she hadn't even bothered to brush her hair. I noticed we had an additional horse with Brigit on her own. I couldn't help but smile as Hait helped me mount his horse. He took his place behind me and I comfortably leaned into him. I looked back to where Gerald was standing, sure he was staring at me. I smiled and waved, and he waved back.

CHAPTER 9

Under normal circumstances, a ward of the crown would have been required to serve as lady-in-waiting to the Queen, but since William Rufus had no wife or was even betrothed, he had assigned the daily management of the household to me. I was happy to do it as it filled my days with such variety, I never got bored.

William kept very few women in his service, even traditionally female positions were filled by handsome young men, including the head cook and chambermaids became chamber men. The only position not occupied by a young man was that of laundress but only because we couldn't find anyone good enough for William who was very particular with his clothing.

Even with the threat of civil war, William didn't hesitate to spend the kingdom's fortune on furniture imported from Italy and clothing from Paris instead of fortifying his military. He was living a more lavish and wasteful life than any king in history.

He demanded the finest Asian silks, Egyptian cottons, and exotic furs from every corner of the world. His boots were made from the skins of crocodile, ostrich, and arapaima, and his royal armor was inlaid with copper, silver, and gold and adorned with the rarest of jewels. No expense was spared to flaunt his extravagance.

Portraits of the King hung on almost every wall depicting him in a familiar way only taller, thinner and less red in the face. Not one depicted the chubby red-faced tyrant that he was. His reflection would be recorded in history as a grand idea rather than reality.

Colorful silks and linens were hung from windows and draped over tables in common areas, decorations that would be more appropriate in a bed chamber than a place to conduct the King's business.

His fascination with bright colors and beautiful things extended to how the people around him were to present themselves. I was dressed in the finest gowns and jewelry handpicked by William himself. Even the lowliest servants were dressed in bright vivid colors with puff and lace instead of the gray tunics found in a normal royal household. William surrounded himself with adolescents brought in from Paris or young men with soft faces from the surrounding kingdom. Only the men-at-arms contained any ruffians.

William's dispute with Robert over the crown was less of a threat with Henry in his service. As long as Henry allied with him, he allowed us to maintain our relationship and promised we could marry but never set a date. It seemed as he used the leverage against each of us. There were days when William was especially cruel, I would beg Henry to run away somewhere and start our lives together.

"We will have a life together, I promise, but I will not live like a pauper when I was born son of a King. William will assign me a post where we can live in peace," he said.

"If he doesn't run the kingdom into poverty. He just returned from Italy with five more young men. How will I keep them all employed? Whenever there is too much idle time, there is trouble."

"Can you send some away?"

"That is not how it works," I say, "William decides when they go, not I."

"William is a strange man; he was a strange boy that my father doted on far too much. I do wonder what he could have said to convince my father to award him the crown over Robert. The only thing I remember was the death of our brother Charles. My father blamed Robert."

"I thought he drown."

"Yes, but Robert was with him. William swore to my father Charles called for help and Robert did nothing."

"Was that true?"

"I was too young at the time, but Robert swears to me, he never heard Charles cry out and when he noticed him floating in the lake, drug him out but he was already dead."

"Your father never forgave Robert?"

"Honestly, I never knew he blamed him, but it is the only reason Robert recalls that could have turned our father against him."

"I need to get the house ready for the evening," I said standing.

"I will see you later tonight," Henry said also standing kissing me tenderly on the cheek.

I went directly to the kitchen making sure the meal was underway. I took a handful of candles and placed them in holders down each hall and strategically around the castle. I would send an attendant to light them as soon as we had kindled the fires.

It was the young son of Purgis who wheeled in the coals, this evening. He was a slight boy barely able to carry the bucket. I led him into William's chamber where William sat in an overstuffed chair. His cheeks were a bright red indicating he was already well into the wine.

I stood by the door and watched the boy nervously struggle with the bucket of coals when William kicked up the side of the carpet, so it created a ledge. I didn't have time to call out the warning before the boy reached the unexpected bump in the carpet, the pail flew from his arms. I instinctively reached to catch the boy to keep him from falling into the coals that now smoldered across the carpet.

"Boy!" William screamed. "Look what you have done."

"It was an accident," I said softly. The boy and I were both on the floor. I knew it was no accident, but I also knew not to challenge William.

"This carpet is one of a kind. It cannot be replaced." William stood above us and lifted the boy by his shirt collar. The boy stayed silent, but tears formed in the corners of his eyes.

"Guards!" he yelled. Two men who were just outside the door appeared instantly.

"I'm sorry," the boy said in a tiny voice.

William ignored the boy and spoke to the guards. "Put him in the tower."

"He's just a boy," I said softly, and instantly regretted my words when the King's boot found my soft middle, taking the breath from me.

"Clean this up," he said to me as I lay on the floor trying to catch my breath. "And find some coal for the fire."

Fortunately, one of the stewards had witnessed what happened and had already found a fireplace that the boy had already delivered coal to. The young steward quietly started the fire as I struggled to roll the carpet, extinguishing the embers while holding my aching ribs. One of the guards led the boy out by the arm while the other waited for instruction. William didn't even try to conceal his sly smirk.

"Bring his father," he told the other guard who quickly disappeared.

With the help of a few of the men, I was able to remove the burned carpet and find a suitable replacement. William continued to drink wine while watching us and laughing as he recounted the boy's fall to one of his men.

After the evening meal, Purgis was presented to the King.

"What took so long?" William asked the guard, initially ignoring Purgis.

"He was deep in the wood," the guard said.

"Do you know why you are here?" William asked the small man.

"I was told my son is in your custody," he said.

"I have been advised that your taxes are late again, Purgis," William said.

"It is only that the taxes have increased, and the hunters have crossed from the royal forest into my lands to hunt stags without paying. But winter is coming, and houses will require charcoal. I am confident the taxes will be satisfied soon." Purgis had inherited most of the great forest from his father, who inherited it from his father. He lived in a simple cottage deep in the forest and made his living as the royal Charcoal Burner, which under William was becoming harder as the taxes on his land increased.

"That might have been good enough before your son destroyed a priceless carpet with his inattention."

"Where is my son?" Purgis asked, his head bowed low.

"He will remain in the tower until the debt is paid."

"I have no way to pay, my Lord."

"But you do," William said, "the forest you own will barely cover the cost of the damage caused by your son but if you transfer your lands to the kingdom, I will forgive all of the debt."

"I cannot survive without the trees to supply charcoal. My family will starve."

"Not my problem but I will let you stay on my property in order that you may still serve the castle. However, if you use any of the charcoal for another source, I will consider it theft and you will hang."

Purgis looked around the room, finally settling his attention on me, but I could do nothing. I was as helpless as anyone else in the room.

"As you wish, my Lord," he said. "May I collect my son?"

"Not tonight. I think I will wait for the assignment to be complete. I will send Henry tomorrow with the documents."

William was obviously very proud of himself. He had just stolen property held for generations and the living it provided for the family with a simple trick. I believed this had been his plan from the moment the boy had arrived with the coal. He had always coveted Purgis's land in the New Forest as it butted up next to his favorite hunting grounds, and now they were his without paying one piece of silver.

The next morning, Henry and I loaded several horses with supplies and retrieved the young son of Purgis from the tower. We didn't have permission to take the child, but no one questioned us. The King would not give him a second thought now that he owned the entirety of the New Forest.

When we arrived, Purgis looked like a different man. He stood tall and confident. I had to let go of the boy as he jumped from the horse into his father's welcoming arms.

"I wasn't bad, Papa. It was an accident."

"I know, son, this burden isn't on your shoulders," his father said, holding his son close. Then he looked at Henry. Their eyes met, and there was clearly an understanding between them. Henry held the rolled parchment, and Purgis simply nodded his head. There was no concern in his face. I didn't understand.

"Go find your mama, and take the Lady," he told his son, and the boy led me around the house, past the metal cart Purgis used to transport the coal. We found the young woman in a roughly built overhang. She was heavy with child, busy dipping candles into a pot of melted beeswax.

"My Lady," she acknowledged me, as her son held her around her waist crying uncontrollably.

"Oh, son, don't cry so. You're nearly a man," she told him.

"He has been through quite an ordeal," I said, "I am sorry I could not be of more assistance."

She looked weary. I was sure the violet circles under her eyes were from worry and lack of sleep caused by the King.

"I'm sure you did what you could, my Lady," she said.

But did I? William was such a cruel king, and I had been playing along for my own survival. I never stood up to him or challenged him.

On our journey home, I had to speak out. "The fire was no accident," I told Henry.

"I have no doubt," he said.

"William tripped the boy on purpose, I saw it myself."

"He was looking for a way to confiscate the forest. I heard him speak of his plans for a hunting lodge weeks ago," Henry admitted.

"There has to be a way to stop him," I said out loud. "Oh, Henry, forgive my outburst against your brother."

"Be careful not to sound treasonous, Nesta."

"I try, but he will never let us marry. I would rather face death than live my life without you," I said.

"You must keep your feelings secret, Nesta. William has lost even the most loyal supporters. His reign may come to an end in the near future, but the time must be right," Henry said looking at me seriously.

"Is there a plot against him?"

"You must not ask such a question or think past this event. I need you to promise to keep your feelings private. Do not share anything with anyone."

"I promise," I said.

"Just trust me and believe that everything will work out."

Even though Henry had not inherited any land from his father and was at his brother's mercy, he had made himself invaluable to his brother. He was quite talented in money management and served as seneschal to the King. His brother trusted him to keep things under control which was a challenge especially with the King's extravagant lifestyle that could easily deplete the royal treasury but somehow Henry managed to keep control.

Henry was vigilant in his duties and tried discreetly to reign in his brother's expenditures. William's usual solution was to increase the financial commitments of his already suffering earldoms and major landholders. In addition to increasing the amount of the financial tributes from landholders, he also reduced military support to outside countries. He kept his forces close in case his brother Robert decided to move against him from Normandy. His favor with the church was also suffering, both for his flamboyant lifestyle and his decreased financial support.

With the lands secured, William wasted no time in producing plans for a new hunting lodge assigning Henry to oversee its construction. William made a new promise with Henry that he would allow us finally to marry at the completion of the lodge.

In the meantime, William didn't care if we slept as husband and wife. Our sins were our own. His were more egregious in the eyes of the church. We were at the King's mercy, so I continued to do everything possible to stay in his good graces.

One evening, when I took him his wine, he invited me to sit.

"Do you have a progress update?"

"It is coming along, I hear. Henry said the roof has been installed, my Lord."

"I plan to take a ride to witness the progress myself," he said, signaling me to take move to the seat in front of him. I could read his moods and knew what pleased him. As I gained his confidence, he indulged me as if I was a younger sister.

"I look forward to the taste of fresh venison upon your return." I smiled sweetly, knowing that though a woman's wiles had no effect on him, flattering his hunting ability always did.

"I have heard stories of a great stag roaming the forest. He is said to be twice the size of any seen before. I intend to make him my first rack in the lodge."

"I hear the barons are envious of such a grand building and eager to find out who you may invite in your first official hunt."

"They all hope to be the first do they?"

"It is all anyone is talking about," I said watching him smile at the thought of others wanting to be the chosen one.

One thing William loved was gossip and I always kept a bit on hand to pass to him. Sometimes I even had to make it a bit juicer so he would be entertained.

"I hear Bishop Flambard was caught with a woman," I said watching his response.

"Who cares," he said rolling his eyes.

"You will not believe what I heard about Brigit today," I

said.

"Please indulge me," he said.

"A farmer's wife caught her husband in the hay on top of Brigit, but she didn't say a thing. Later the evening when she was asleep, the woman cut all of Brigit's curls clean off. When Brigit woke and saw her locks on the ground, she went into a fury lashing out at everyone nearby. One of the guards picked her up and threw her into the moat. But it wasn't the clean side. She was thrown into the latrine flow side."

William started to laugh so hard he bent in half. I filled his cup with ale two times before he regained his composure.

I wasn't able to keep Brigit by my side in Williams court. William couldn't stand her and sent her fifty miles away to Westminster as a housemaid. At first, she was furious with me, though I had no control over the decision, but I traveled to Westminster to visit as often as I could.

"If that girl didn't provide so much entertainment, I would ship her right back to Ireland," he said, "I only wish I could have seen her covered in shit."

CHAPTER 10

Scotland was another country deeply affected by William's desires. He continued to increase the tributes demanded from the country and ignored the peace carefully negotiated by his father with King Malcolm that guaranteed Scotland's independence from English rule.

King William Rufus began to expand his kingdom, often invading other's property but when constructing Carlisle Castle in Cumbria, which itself didn't cross the border but was so close to the line that when the English barons began setting up their earldoms around the new castle, their construction was a clear encroachment of Scottish held lands.

When Malcom ordered them to remove themselves, the earls claimed that the land had been granted to them by the King. It became quite clear that King William had no interest in maintaining peace with his neighbors to the north and instead of negotiating, raised forces to enforce the barons' claims.

Instead of a direct advance toward Malcom, William carefully constructed a skirmish where Malcolm had no chance and was killed. This time, I overheard his plan myself and realized the way my father died was too similar. I had no longer had any doubt that William was responsible for my own father's death.

Within weeks, another political pawn arrived in Winchester. The King didn't even bother greeting the girl and the small entourage that accompanied her into the castle. Like most things he considered unimportant, he left this official task up to me.

Edith, the daughter of King Malcom and Queen Margret,

appeared fragile as she climbed out of the carriage that transported her from the only home she had ever known. Her mother had disappeared, lost to depression and committed to a nunnery to live out her life.

I watched Edith walk slowly toward us, I couldn't tell what she looked like as she was completely veiled, dressed in a plain white frock that hid her shape and was devoid of any embellishments.

I walked silently with her to the chamber next to mine, opened the door and sat next to her on the bed.

"I am Nesta, Princess of Deheubarth," I said. "My chamber is right next door so if you need anything..."

"I will not have any need," she said softly, "except to be left alone."

I took my leave silently, leaving her sitting motionless on the side of the bed.

Later when I went to check on her, I could hear her weeping as I put my ear to her door. I considered this an opportunity to reach out to her, as we found ourselves in similar circumstances.

"May I enter?" I asked, knocking softly on the heavy wooden door.

"Enter." Edith's voice was soft like a child's. I walked in and saw her sitting in a high-backed chair near the window. She motioned for me to sit next to her as if I were one of her ladies and not her equal. I took my seat realizing she was probably still in shock from her ordeal.

"How are you feeling?" I asked her.

"I'm worried for my mother," she said. Her long dark hair hung loose as if she was ready to brush it but had given up.

"Where is she?" I asked.

"She lived here, you know," she said turning to me showing me soft brown eyes slightly red-rimmed from crying.

"Here?"

"At Windsor. She was the daughter of the Briton King, and when the Normans took this land, my father rescued my mother and brought her under his protection. She was raised in Winchester. It was William's grandfather who stole the crown from my family." Tears formed in her eyes but didn't fall.

"Does she know you are here?"

"She is inconsolable since the death of my father, and only speaks to God. She wouldn't even travel to see me before I left Wilton Abbey, where I lived with my sister under my aunt's care. My father promised to send me back to my mother, but now he is gone." Her tears now let loose. "I will never see my mother or my sister again," she said, starting to sob loudly. I wasn't sure what to do. I took her in my arms and let her bury her head into my shoulder. I kept my arms around her, gently rocking, and trying to provide comfort as a mother might to her daughter. We were close to the same age, but she seemed much younger.

While she had lived a pious life behind abbey walls, I had already experienced some of life's hardest lessons. I thought about the child I had lost. I now hoped to have an opportunity to start the life I had dreamed of with Henry. Somehow, with this girl's presence, I might be able to convince William that I am of no consequence.

"We must face the destiny laid upon us by our ancestors," I said confidently. "We must simply face it with as much courage as we can find within us. Just remember you were born for this," I said, watching her face change as she wiped her eyes and stood up.

"You're right," she said. "I find myself on this path, and I shall follow it to wherever it leads." I smiled at her and took a brush from her side table. She turned away, allowing me to brush her thick black hair and form one long plait from the top of her head to the center of her back. She was a beautiful girl. I stood in front of her and watched her eyes brighten.

After she put on a proper gown, we walked side by side to the dining hall. She was dazed with amazement, for every hallway and staircase was adorned with portraits or detailed tapestries. The windows were covered with colorful silk and lace that she needed to touch as we walked past. I imagined she didn't walk on carpet shipped from India and Egypt when she lived at the abbey. I watched her face as she examined every small table that held ornate vases, ivory statues, or all the other extraordinary ornaments William surrounded himself with.

"I've never seen anything like this," she said.

"Our host has exotic taste," I said, as we were greeted by several young men dressed identically in orange and blue tunics with white ruffled sleeves over tight black britches. They wore black boots that came almost to their knees and had a shine that could only have been achieved by rubbing them for hours with pig's oil.

The dining hall itself was the grandest exhibit of William's need for show. Edith stopped short as she entered, and I watched her stare at each stag head. Boar heads stared at us with beady glass eyes and curled gray tusks. There was a great white owl, several white-tailed eagles, harriers, goshawks, ospreys, and even an ostrich, all expertly preserved by the royal taxidermist. In between the stuffed animals hung great tapestries depicting hunting scenes with horses and dogs, and of course, portraits of our King. "You'll get used to it," I said, remembering my shock the first time I saw the hall.

William and Henry were both already seated at the long table, but only Henry stood to greet us. The young attendants pulled out our chairs and poured our wine before they began to deliver platters of meat and bread. I watched the silent interaction between Henry and Edith. Henry was so handsome and his smile so penetrating that Edith blushed from his attention.

"Have you had the opportunity to walk the castle, my Lady?" Henry asked Edith.

"No, my Lord, I have been unpacking in my room," she said shyly. "But the path we took to the dining hall was quite magnificent."

William smiled, and continued to eat what looked like a full pork shoulder. There was an attendant on each side waiting to slice the meat or pour his ale.

"My dear brother has spared no expense in surrounding himself with only the finest," Henry said, loud enough to get William's attention.

"Are you questioning the King's discretion, brother?" William asked with a laugh.

"Absolutely not, my King. I would never question the wise purchase of a dining chair equal in cost to the finest warhorse," Henry said.

"Why would you need another warhorse?" William asked. "Now, a good hunting hound would be a different story."

"I would like to explore the castle more fully, my Lord," her voice low, as she failed to disguise her nervousness.

"And I would be happy to show you through it," Henry said.

"I'll bet you would," William again spoke sarcastically, without looking away from his next bite.

"It seems well fortified," Edith said nervously, without thinking of what she was saying. She then remembered to breathe, and Henry was further entertained. He looked into her dark eyes, and with a wide smile seemed to forget I was in the room.

"This castle is designed to protect its greatest asset," William said, looking at us all.

"And what is that?" Henry asked, looking at his brother.

"It's Queen, of course," William said, before his attentions were again focused on his plate.

Henry and I both turned in disbelief toward William, hardly believing what we just heard. William was obviously up to something. He looked back at us and smiled as he took a bite of a fresh roll stuffed with raspberry preserves.

Edith seemed not to notice our shock, but it would be a surprise if she hadn't heard the rumors about William. Henry ignored William and returned his focus to Edith.

"You might not remember," Henry said, "but we played together as children. You were just a tiny little thing and I was twice your age. You chased me around the courtyard. I fell over a rock and you sat on my head."

Appalled and embarrassed, Edith insisted, "I could not have done such a thing. Not only was I brought up correctly, but my mother would never have allowed such play."

"I'm afraid it's true, Princess. Your mother was distracted, and your brothers were watching over you. I remember it quite vividly. You sat on my head," Henry said.

"I refuse to acknowledge such an act. Besides," she continued, "I would have remembered your face, and I do not."

"Of course, you would not remember this face," he laughed. "It was quite changed after a child sat on my head." Edith's faced changed from insulted to a sweet smile and they both began to laugh. Henry had been successful in breaking through Edith's shell, and now he was enjoying getting to know the girl raised in a nunnery.

I had had enough of Henry's flirtatious manner in front of me. It was more painful than I could bear, but I resolved it as possibly a ruse to thwart William somehow. For the rest of the meal, William and Henry treated me as if I was invisible. They competed for Edith's attention like it was a new toy.

Finally, William's favorite attendant of the day took a position next to him, indicating William's intention to retire as he did after every meal.

"Tomorrow we will have a hunt in your honor, Princess," William announced, as he stood, assisted by the young man dressed extravagantly in a rich blue velvet cloak with light brown fur cuffs. "Time to celebrate," he said as he walked out the door.

"Celebrate what?" I said to Henry, who was looking uncomfortable.

"I do not know what things live in my brother's head," Henry said. I could tell he was worried, so I was also concerned.

Later, when we were alone, I asked Henry, "Are you in love with her?"

"Don't be ridiculous, I am merely observing my brother as he executes a plan. If he took this woman as a wife, he would have better control over the English. It is a perfect solution to an impossible political problem. His heirs would have the royal bloodline of her mother and the Scottish loyalty of her father, satisfying the people in both countries united under his crown."

"Poor girl."

It was two Sundays since Edith's arrival to Winchester and the hall was full of guests. William decided on a formal dinner as usual sparing no expense. His guest list included Archbishop Anselm of Canterbury; Bishop Randolph Flambard of Durham; Sir Walter, the Earl of Buckingham and his wife Ermengarde; Sir Robert, the Earl of Leicester and his wife Adelin; Sir Gilbert de Clare, the Earl of Pembroke; Robert Montgomery from Shrewsbury; and Walter Tyrel.

I had arranged the seating carefully. I put the Bishop and Archbishop close enough to the King so as not to be offended but not next to each other where they could be interpreted as conspiring against the King. I sat directly across from William to keep an eye out for any displeasure, ensuring that I could make corrections.

Henry was assigned the seat next to his brother but moved himself between the two wives at the farthest end and out of my view. Though I couldn't see him, I found comfort in the sound of his familiar laugh. He loved being the center of the attention, especially among the ladies. I sat Edith next to me both as a comfort to her, and to keep her well away from Henry. The table was full, and the King was in an especially good mood.

As a result of his love of hunting, the castle was always well stocked with venison, rabbit, and wild boar, all of which was piled high on the table in front of us. The dinner conversation, led by the King, included details of how the very meal in front of us had been stalked and killed. He even described and took great delight in reproducing the scream of the wounded animal. I heard one of the women gasp and watched Edith's face turn pale as he described the look in a wounded doe's eyes as he took a knife to her throat. Both Edith and I gently pushed our plates away from us.

Except for the gruesome hunting stories, the overall conversation was light and enjoyable. The dinner was a success, and the King would be pleased with my efforts. Just as I let the contentment of the evening wash over me, the King stood to make an announcement. The conversation stopped so everyone could hear what the King had to say.

"Thank you all for a most enjoyable evening. I feel well served by my people, and I am aware that uncertainty about succession has been a cause of concern. It is time to announce the promise of a true heir as I have chosen a wife." He lifted his golden goblet inlaid with rubies and sapphires for a toast.

As expected, the guests were frozen as if the Hag of Hell had suddenly appeared and cast a spell upon them. I finally broke the deafening silence.

"My King?" I asked softly.

"Not you, fool! I wouldn't touch my brother's consort, no matter your pedigree," he said cruelly. I felt my face turn red as the anger rose.

"I certainly wasn't suggesting that" I said.

"The Princess Edith of Scotland will be my wife, the next Queen of England," he said confidently. I heard Edith gasp and I reached under the table to put my hand on her trembling leg. How could this brute announce such a thing at a table full of guests like it had just occurred to him, without properly notifying the intended bride in advance?

"This is great news, my King," said Bishop Randolph, the keeper of the royal seal. He stood and signaled the rest of us to stand for a toast. We all took the cue and held our wine and ale high above our heads as he said, "To the King."

"To the King," we all repeated in unison, taking obligatory sips of our drinks.

"To an heir," Bishop Randolph raised his cup again.

"To an heir," we all repeated, again raising our cups.

As we sat back down, the conversation among the guests continued without mentioning the obvious. Not one person who sat at the table had any doubt of our King's proclivities and had accepted the fact, especially the Archbishop whose council always included the need for a queen.

I was confused, and it was hard for me to believe William could provide an heir to England. I thought I was used to his abuse, but William was not finished with me yet.

"Are you not in agreement with my choice, Princess Nesta?" he asked smiling. The room again went silent. William's voice had changed from the merry tone of his announcement to accusatory as he addressed me.

"Don't take this wrong, my King," I started.

"Don't," I heard Henry say aloud, and could feel him approach me from behind.

"It's just that I imagined, well, it is difficult to—" I suddenly wished I had remained silent. William's face twisted and turned the same putrid color of a rose petal just before it falls from the stem.

It was too late to pray for mercy. William picked up the meat pie in front of him and hurled it across the table, barely missing Lady Adelin, Earl Robert's wife. It was lucky that no other food was within his immediate reach, or I may have ended up wearing it.

"For your information, young lady," William started to smile, "every marriage has a political consequence. Even a peasant hopes for an advantageous union, and that, my dear, is why you and my brother," William motioned toward us with the drunken hand holding his goblet spilling some of its contents on the bishop, "and your bastard son will never be safe as long as I am King." I gasped, just now learning that William not only knew of the existence of my son but now made sure that all these people had the same information, my chance for a proper marriage seemed to have disappeared. "How do you think it was so easy to convince my father to reduce Henry's claim to the throne. He will never be good enough," said William, continuing his rampage.

"My King!" Henry pleaded.

"Sit down, brother." William continued looking down

the table at each guest as if he was talking directly to each of them, piecing out his announcement with ire. "Henry is nothing but a boy who chases virgins from every part of the land. My dear lady here believes she bore the only bastard of my brother's seed. But I will tell you that there are so many that the coffers of the kingdom would be empty if I paid every claim that has been presented to me."

I shut my eyes tightly, hoping that I would disappear, but instead felt the eyes of these patrons focusing on me. I knew it was time to show strength, so I refused to cry. When I opened my eyes, with one eyebrow raised, I stared right back at my silent accusers. William threw his goblet, splashing the last of his wine onto the nearest guests. He stormed from the room, leaving us to digest his revelation.

"What were you thinking, you foolish girl?" Bishop Randolph shook his head in disapproval. Henry moved closer to me and held out his hand to guide me away from the table. I bowed my head to avoid looking at the guests and allowed Henry to silently deliver me to my chamber.

"What are we going to do?" I asked Henry.

"Just trust me," he said, and kissed my hot cheek. He didn't seem as upset as I thought he should be.

"What about everything he said? Is it true, do you have other children?" I asked.

"You must trust me," he whispered. "Things will work out."

"My life is ruined," I said.

With tear-filled eyes I curled onto my bed like a child and wished my mother was nearby. I felt abandoned and alone. This was the evening I planned to tell Henry that I carried another child of his. Now I could not bear the thought of revealing it without some assurance we would marry, which was beginning to seem even more unlikely.

CHAPTER 11

When I woke hearing the house busier than usual, I looked out my chamber window and saw several carts piled high with supplies. The grooms were tying the hunting hounds to the saddled horses and men were laughing. The commotion was welcome, as it meant the King was headed to his new lodge, where he hopefully would have a successful hunt. Even better if he could find the giant stag that had become his obsession. Henry came up behind me and wrapped his arms around my middle. He placed his head next to mine looking out.

"Will you send me off?" he asked.

"You are really going hunting with your brother?" I asked, surprised that after the events of the evening before, Henry would have been willing to be in the company of his brother.

"Of course," he said. "I wouldn't miss this for the world."

I walked next to Henry to the courtyard, but kept out of William's view, fearing more of his abuse.

"I need my horse," William said to the groom who was standing by for just such an order.

"It has been almost a month since I've been able to hunt and today is the perfect day. The stags will be encouraged by the sweet new growth, and dizzy with the temptation of a new young doe." I wasn't sure who he was talking to, but his eyes were focused on Henry.

The brothers Robert and Gilbert de Clare rode through the gate with Walter Tyrel close behind.

"Those are fine hounds," William said. "I have never seen one so pure white." Walter was well known for the quality of dogs he bred.

"My Lord, this hound is delivered to you as a gift today. He is a rare breed from Mongolia," Walter said.

William was pleased and leaned down to the hound, holding the back of his hand to the dog's nose. The animal sniffed but stood at attention.

"Release," William said, and the great white dog pulled at his tether, eager to run. "Heel," William said, causing the dog to transform back into a calm state. We could all tell how pleased William was with such a gift. His face lit up with all the beautiful animals around him.

"This would make a perfect portrait," he said to his steward.

"The artist will be prepared upon your return, my Lord." The steward bowed low.

"My Lord," Gilbert spoke up. "I, too, have brought you a gift today."

"It is not the day of my birth, is it?" William said with a hearty laugh but looked overjoyed.

Gilbert unwrapped the large bundle exposing six perfect arrows. "These arrows were specially designed for you. If there is a man on this earth who will take down the great stag, it is our King. These arrows are guaranteed to pierce the flesh of the greatest of beasts."

"I am honored by this gift," William said. He packed four of the arrows into his side holder. The arrows were too broad to fit all of them in, so he looked at Walter Tyrel and handed him two of the arrows.

"My Lord?" Walter asked, not quite knowing what he should do.

"You are the only other hunter here worth his salt. It will be a miracle if Henry even lets an arrow go. He never had much taste for hunting." Henry's face didn't change. He wasn't going to react to his brother's taunts.

"Let's get on with it," Henry said loudly, and looked toward Walter who gave Henry a small nod. Henry turned to find me partially hidden behind a cart. He smiled and blew a kiss as he mounted his horse. I watched the group disappear out the gate with William leading in a fine gold baroque tunic, most inappropriate for a hunt, but typical for William who was far from practical. Robert and Gilbert de Clare followed directly behind him. Henry and Walter seemed to keep a purposeful distance from the rest of the group. I watched the silvery white hounds, two at each side of the King as if they were ghost-marching their master into the gates of heaven. William was correct when he said it would be a great portrait.

Early the next morning, to everyone's surprise, the hunting party rode back through the very gate they departed. Henry was in the lead followed by Gilbert and Robert de Clare all moving at a slow trot. Walter Tyrel and the King were not with them.

Unprepared for the early return, attendants scrambled to gather enough help to greet them. When they saw the King was absent, they lost their sense of urgency and just a few gathered at the front gate. The others continued to go about their business. I took my position near the front, eager to see Henry's face. As soon as the men were close enough, I could see by the look on his face that something was horribly wrong. "Call the Archbishop," he said to the steward. "Quickly."

"Where is the King?" I asked, and he turned to look behind him. The small party that had gathered followed his gaze. We all spotted the charcoal burner's cart pulled by the mare and led by Purgis himself. We watched in silence as he made his way toward us.

"The King is dead," Henry said. I heard someone gasp behind me, but I just froze, measuring my emotions. A confused mixture of panic and joy washed over me.

The Archbishop arrived with several monks. He did not ask Purgis anything and instructed the monks to take the body. Henry led us all into the great hall. He didn't care who was in the room. He wanted to share the events that led to his brother's death.

"We were all tired from too much ale the night before, but

William insisted on an early start. He released the hounds as soon as there was enough light in the sky. Then Robert sounded the huntsman's horn." We all looked at Robert who sat across from Henry and next to his brother. He looked to Henry and his brother and took a deep breath.

"Walter and King William went on ahead of us following the baying of the hounds," Robert said.

"We circled around the other side, hoping to cut the stag off as he attempted to escape the hounds," Henry added. "Apparently, the stag was cornered, and it looks like William didn't wait for us and made the move to the other side. We had already stopped where the path ended to wait for a signal. We waited for a long time. Finally, I left my horse and walked to the place in the forest where I thought they might be. It was too quiet. I signaled my position with a low whistle, and Walter's call led me to him at the foot of Fryen Hill. William was lying near a large oak tree with an arrow straight through his heart. Walter was kneeling next to him visibly shaking."

"It sounds like an unfortunate accident," the Archbishop said, "and it will be recorded as such."

"It was an accident," Henry said, wiping the sweat from his forehead with his hand. "Walter had the shot and as his arrow left his bow, the stag moved. The arrow glanced off the oak, changing its course to the exact spot where William stood. I witnessed the arrow's mark on the tree."

"No one is at fault," the Archbishop said.

"Where is Walter?" I asked.

"I'm not sure. He was inconsolable. I went to get Purgis to help and when I returned, he was gone," Henry said.

Henry and the Archbishop organized the castle and unceremoniously arranged William's burial that very evening.

The news of William's death traveled fast, and the details reported as a horrible accident stayed intact. I suspected the truth was known only by the few that were there. I did not shed a tear for our King, but worried about the consequences to the country. I had no opportunity to speak with Henry, as he moved quickly to gain the support of influential men in the kingdom, once again denying Robert his rightful claim to the crown. Before the news had even reached his brother, Henry had taken his place on the throne, and had complete control of all the assets.

Henry wasted no time reorganizing the castle, quickly dismissed the excess staff and assigned influential Lords to key positions in return for their pledged support. He awarded his most loyal supporters houses and land. He even returned to Purgis his land in the New Forest. These men would all support him as the rightful King. Even the Archbishop was in favor of Henry as King, especially when Henry accepted his recommendation of a wife.

"How could you do this to me?" I screamed.

"My mother bore a commander, not a soldier," he said, "I must do whatever is necessary to fulfill my destiny. The people will stand with me with Edith by my side. Nothing changes between you and me," he said, trying to calm me.

"Nothing changes? Everything changes!" I said loudly.

"I don't think you understand politics," he said. "It is my destiny to rule England. It was always my destiny."

"I am with child, Henry," I said, defeated, with tears running down both my cheeks. I touched my middle and shook my head. Henry stood looking at me as if he didn't understand the words.

"How can that be?"

"Honestly, I am surprised it didn't happen sooner," I said.

Henry stayed silent as the blood drained from his face. He turned his back on me and for a few moments stayed still. Finally, he left my chamber, silently closing the door behind him.

Henry had broken my heart once again. After all this time waiting for my life to begin, I had been reduced to a King's consort. I tried several times to speak with him, but he refused to see me.

The only choice I had was to speak with Edith. If I told her the situation, she might understand and speak with Henry in my favor. I was sure she would rather be returned to Scotland than be married to a man she barely knew but I was wrong.

I knocked softly.

"Come," Edith called.

"I just came to see how you were doing," I said sitting on a low bench facing her as she ran a comb through her long dark hair.

"I haven't seen you lately," she said.

"I've remained in my room, not sure of my position any longer. Am I now your lady?"

She looked at me without changing her expression. "I shall not tolerate my husband's whore under my own roof," she said without even blinking.

"I am not Henry's whore," I said standing up barely holding my balance as I stepped back.

"I am not blind, and you have confided in me many times of your wish to marry Henry, but he will marry me, and I think there is no room for you or your bastard child running through this castle." She pointed her comb at my midsection. "I will be too focused on producing a proper heir to the kingdom to be able to monitor your activities."

"How can you be so cruel, I thought we were friends," I said as tears ran down my cheeks.

"You were right, Nesta, I too have a destiny. My ancestors were the Britons who inhabited this land only two generations ago and now will be returned through my heir."

"But you are also the daughter of the Scottish King who was likely taken down by King William." I said.

"William is dead, and Henry will bring our lands to peace. The pope himself has blessed this union. It is God's will."

I was stunned at the harshness of her words, but she obviously believed her chastity put her above me. The door to my future was again slammed shut.

I returned to my chamber and fell face first onto my bed screaming deep into the cotton to muffle my pain. I cried until there were no tears left and my eyes burned. Finally, exhausted, I slept holding my hands on my belly unsure of the destiny of this child. My fear is that Henry would confiscate it too.

I did not attend the wedding or any of the celebrations surrounding the grand affair but could hear the festivities continue until the early hours of the next day.

I imagined the consummation had been witnessed and I wondered if he told her he loved her. I wanted to cry but there were no more tears left.

The House had hardly settled when there was a soft knock at my door.

Hoping it was Henry, I swung it open, but it was just an attendant.

"Bishop Randolf requests your presence in the church as soon as you can," he said handing me a small scroll. I didn't bother reading it but got dressed. Maybe Henry would be waiting for me at the church.

It took me longer than normal to get ready since my hair hadn't been attended to for a few days and I had no lady's help.

"Your insolence is intolerable," the Bishop said without even looking up. I looked for Henry, but he wasn't anywhere in sight.

"My insolence?" I asked.

"You walk around here like you have no sin."

"Where is Henry?"

"In my opinion, the Queen should have you locked in a cell out of sight, but her Christian heart has found a solution," he said.

"What are you talking about?"

The smile on his face frightened me as he led me out the back door to the awaiting litter carrying my two chests. He opened the door and pointed in.

"Where are you taking me?" I asked.

"Get in," he ordered, "or I will take great pleasure in locking you up myself."

I reluctantly climbed in and took a seat, but I unfortunately wouldn't be traveling alone as he climbed in right behind me. The litter was small, and I disliked being so near the Bishop whose breath smelled of sour ale.

It took the full day and into the night to reach our destination which happened to be Pembroke Castle where Gerald greeted us as if he had been expecting our arrival.

Gerald had remained the Castilian of Pembroke and had always been a loyal supporter of Henry. I saw that this might be a solution, returning me to my home in Wales, but why would I be escorted by the Bishop instead of the normal men-at-arms? The question was answered when the Bishop handed Gerald a scroll with the King's seal. Gerald silently read it, looked up at me confused, and read it again.

Recognizing my confusion, he asked, "Are you aware of the contents of this letter?"

"No, my Lord. I was whisked away this very morning without even the courtesy of a cloak," I said.

He handed me the scroll. The Bishop reached to snatch it from my hand and Gerald pushed his hand away. "Let her read it."

I opened the scroll fully and could tell right away it was the King's decree, complete with his seal. I was to be wed to Gerald, and my dowry was to be the lands of my father. It was signed by Henry, the King of England.

"I don't understand," I said.

"Foolish girl," the Bishop said. "You will be wed today." I looked to Gerald for support, but he was as surprised as I was.

"I'm sorry," he said as he recognized the disappointment in my face.

"There is no need to be sorry. I am simply in shock," I said, "Did you know of this plan?"

"No, my Lady. I am also at a disadvantage."

"Can we not wait until I can dress appropriately?" I asked the Bishop.

"It will take place this minute. I have no more time to waste on this nonsense."

"We need witnesses," I said.

Gerald signaled his man to the castle to fetch some witnesses.

"I'm sorry for your misfortune," I said as we waited.

"I will try to be a kind husband," he said.

"Thank you," I said, looking directly into my new husband's eyes where I saw not only kindness but strength, the kind of strength I might be able to count on.

I was relieved when Willa appeared taking me in her meaty arms, "welcome home, my dear."

The Bishop hurried through the ceremony barely giving us time to acknowledge the words. I wasn't even listening and had to be nudged more than once by Willa to answer.

I was married to Gerald of Pembroke not Henry, but I wasn't angry with Henry, who without the decency to wish me well, had simply banished me out the back door. I didn't even curse him that night as I lay my head on my pillow. My future was out of William's hands, and was no longer dictated by Henry. Now is the time I would take control of my own life.

CHAPTER 12

Gerald took his assignment as my husband very seriously. Although we had not consummated our marriage, our life in Pembroke resembled a normal privileged household. The local Welsh inhabitants welcomed me with open arms, and peace became easier as the trust between the locals and the Normans improved with my presence.

There was a certain relief to have my feet back on Welsh soil, breathing Welsh air and surrounded by Welsh people. I was especially happy to have Willa near, she had been a second mother to me, so it was a comforting for such an ally.

"I wish my family was here," I said, "I can almost hear my mother's voice behind me, reminding me to spend time with a needle."

"She would be proud of the woman you have become," Willa said.

"I wish I had never met Henry. It is all my fault my family is gone, and I am alone."

"I'm afraid you had no choice as God had his plans made before you were even born and it is your destiny to be in this moment, and you are not alone," she said patting my middle.

"What is this child's future as a bastard of a King?"

"Don't forget he is also the grandson of a great Welsh King," she said.

"He?"

"I know these things," she said.

"Honestly, I hope for a girl so she will be invisible to the King and I may keep her by my side."

"Whatever this child is, they are blessed by God." Willa

took me in her arms and hugged me. "This is your chance to correct history and take your place in it."

"Thank you, Willa," I said as she released me, and I sat heavily on my favorite chair.

As if he could read my mind, Gerald walked in holding a steaming cup of tea.

"I thought you could use this," he said as he sat on the small bench next to my chair. I accepted the tea eagerly. Willa had quietly left us, picking up some laundry as she left.

"This is exactly what I needed, thank you, Gerald," I said taking a sip testing the temperature. I sat back and closed my eyes, finally able to relax.

"Are you feeling okay?" he asked.

"This child is an active one, so sleep is rare. It seems as soon as I close my eyes, the child decides to do an Irish jig."

"I'm so sorry to bother you, I will leave and let you rest," he said.

"Please no," I said sitting up looking at him. It was a rare thing for Gerald to actually be comfortable near me and I wanted to take this opportunity for an informal conversation. "I would like you to sit with me a bit."

"I see the nursery is almost complete," he said awkwardly.

"It is," I said.

"I have something for you, and I hope it pleases you," he said.

"What is it?"

"I'm afraid you will need to leave that chair," he said standing holding out his arm so I could use it to leverage.

"Well, lead on but I must say it had better be good for me to leave the comfort of that chair."

We walked the short distance to the very next chamber where I had set the nursery.

Gerald opened the door and stood aside as I entered, and before I took even two steps, I froze. Tears welled and fell from my eyes. The same cradle that had held my first child was sitting in middle of the room.

Seeing the tears, Gerald came to face me, "Oh no. I am so sorry, I really thought it would make you happy." I looked at him like it was the first time I'd ever seen him.

"Of course, I am happy," I said falling into his arms as he held me close. I could feel his strength surrounding me.

"Of course, we will move it into your chamber when the child comes," he said still holding me.

"Of course," I said with my head still buried in his chest, "thank you."

I never asked how Gerald knew about the cradle or why he bothered to retrieve it, but I figured Willa may have whispered in his ear.

The cradle wasn't the greatest gift Gerald gave me, but it was the look on his face as he held my son, Henry fitz Henry, in his arms for the first time. Gerald stared at the boy with the love and wonder I had never seen a man display. He wasn't afraid but confident as he held him gently rocking the child. I knew from that moment I would never worry for my son as he had a father.

It had been a long night and I was exhausted but needed to look at my son before I slept. Gerald placed Henry in my open arms. The tiny boy was perfect. His low, raspy cry made me smile. His perfect round face reminded me of his brother Robert, the son I had lost for what seemed like a lifetime ago. I felt a tear roll down my cheek, not sure if it fell for the loss or for the restoration of hope.

For the first time in a long time, I was whole again. I took my eyes from my son just long enough to look at my husband who stood nearby. I saw tears in Gerald's eyes.

"Are you okay?" I asked Gerald.

"He is amazing," he said.

"He is amazing," I said pulling my smock down and placing little Henry's mouth on my nipple to soothe his cries.

Gerald watched me in amazement as the child eagerly suckled.

"I will leave you in capable hands but if you need anything, please call on me."

"I will," I said.

I finally let go of my son and Willa tucked him securely into the cradle next to my bed as my exhaustion finally took hold. It wasn't until Gerald was above me shaking me that I awoke from what I thought to be a deep sleep.

"I was worried for you," he said.

I looked at him, and for the first time his eyes didn't leave mine. I saw true concern.

"I heard you call out. It sounded like you were crying."

It was then I remembered the remnants of my dream in which Henry on a horse with my child in his arms. I didn't feel like exposing this fear to Gerald, so I just said, "It was just a bad dream."

I must have also woken the baby as he began to squirm a bit. I watched Gerald gently
lift Henry from the small bed and bring him to his chest which I just noticed was bare. I was impressed with the tenderness and genuine interest in the child even though it was not his own. I imagined now that I was no longer pregnant, Gerald might expect heirs of his own.

Henry began to fuss which signaled Gerald to hand him to me as I exposed my breast to my son who urgently latched on.

"He is just hungry," I said.

"I will leave you. I was just worried," he said.

"You can hold him anytime," I said as Gerald turned to walk out the door.

"I would like that," he said turning back before he disappeared from the room.

Gerald sent word to Henry that he had a son but fortunately, no response was returned. My sleep was haunted by my biggest fear where Henry appears with that woman and again steals my son.

One evening late into the night, Gerald and I sat up watching our child suffer a great fever. He looked so fragile and red-faced, with his light blonde hair plastered to his head. His breathing was so shallow we both sat silent, listening for the next breath to occur. My heart was breaking. I felt helpless as this fever was taking the lives of many children.

"I would gladly trade my life for the relief of this child's suffering," I said quietly.

Gerald moved to me and on his knees in front of me, took both my hands in his.

"If there is even one angel in heaven, this child will not only recover but will become the fiercest warrior in all of history."

"Is it wrong to wish your son a bishop instead of a warrior?"

"I'm afraid that is every mother's wish," he said smiling, "and every father's fear."

I looked Gerald in his sincere eyes. "You believe in destiny?" I asked, speaking quietly.

"Destiny and fate cannot be changed no matter how much you wish or pray, but faith is a gift that cannot be taken from me," he said.

"Even when you were forced to marry a woman unknown to you until your wedding day?"

"Marriage to you is far from a misfortune. I consider that day the most fortunate day of my whole life." I couldn't help smiling as he spoke, never taking his eyes from mine.

"But you had no choice in the matter," I said.

"The King forced me to marry the most beautiful woman the country has ever known, who happens to be a princess and heir to the Kingdom of Deheubarth. At the risk of treason, I believe the King a fool. I would have relinquished every piece of silver from my treasury, every warhorse in my stable, and pledged land I have yet to own to be granted your hand. I am only a knight in the King's service. There is nothing in this life I have done to deserve you as my wife."

Gerald had never before uttered a word indicating his true feelings toward me. I just assumed he tolerated my presence and was simply fulfilling his duty to the crown. He kissed each of my hands softly causing an unfamiliar stirring in my body, but the moment was interrupted when young Henry cried out.

Both Gerald and I instinctively put our hands on the boy's face.

"I think the fever has broken," I said with relief.

Gerald lifted Henry out of his small bed which instantly soothed him.

"There's my boy," he said smiling in relief.

I smiled watching the two of them. Henry laid his head on Gerald's shoulder and I changed the linens on the small bed. Sensing the activity in the room, the nurse woke from where she had been sleeping in a bed on the other side of the nursery. She put her hand on the baby's head and confirmed what I already knew, Henry was going to be okay.

"It's broke," she said. "Now you two get some rest." She reached for the child hanging on to Gerald, who reluctantly surrendered him to the nurses waiting arms, after kissing him on the head.

Gerald took my hand in his and led me to my chamber door. I was exhausted, relieved, and exhilarated by Gerald's earlier words. As I reached for the handle, Gerald slid his arm to push the door open. He followed me in and pushed the door closed and then pushed my body into the closed door pressing his body against mine. He then pressed his lips to mine before I could object.

The warmth of his lips and the heaviness of his body caused me to wilt. I returned the kiss but his was hungry and I could barely catch my breath causing me to gasp.

"I'm sorry, did I hurt you?" he said backing away. He was always so careful with me, like I was a fragile doll too easily broken.

"No, not at all," I said breathless. "I was just surprised, and pleased,"

"I want you," he whispered.

"I want you, too," I said softly, and pulled him closer, encouraging him to continue.

He reached behind me and guided me around until we reached the edge of the bed. His eyes never left mine, even when he kissed me, he kept his eyes on me.

The hunger I suddenly felt took over and I could hardly wait for Gerald to loosen my ties and remove my dress. He finally stepped back to look at my body, only covered by a flimsy white shift. I felt self-conscious of my body that had now birthed two sons. He might have noticed my concern or was sensitive to my modesty. He lifted me onto the bed and quickly slid off his clothes while still kissing my face and my neck. Before long he moved his mouth over my entire body until, finally, he ended my suffering when he took his wife for the first time.

CHAPTER 13

I no longer suffered in my forced marriage but began to enjoy the relationship between Gerald and me. It became one of friendship and mutual respect. He cared very much for me and I wanted to find room in my heart to love him, but something always tugged at me to reserve that emotional tie.

I listened without judgement as he recounted his strategy against Welsh uprisers, fascinated with his logic. It seemed that Gerald could read a man's heart and judge his actions. He could often settle a dispute without a sword.

Under the Llangernyw Yew, on a small bench, Gerald had crafted for me, I finally confessed my love for my husband.

"It is this day that I find my heart is fully tied to yours. I love you more than words can say. God has delivered you to me when I was broken and under your tender care, I feel restored," I said holding Gerald's hand in mine.

"My dear Nesta, it has been my life's goal to give you comfort and it is more than I have ever hoped that you could return the feelings I have felt for you since the first time I laid eyes on you," he said kneeling in front of me kissing my hand softly.

I could see the familiar kindness in his eyes, and I recognized the desire he held deep. He took me from the bench and laid me on the moss below. I submitted happily as his gentle ways brought me to pleasure so easy.

I felt a tear slip from my eye as he finished and was now on one elbow looking at me.

"What is wrong?" he asked kissing away the tear.

"I am with child," I said calmly. The shock on his face turned quickly to joy like I had never seen. He jumped up and pulled me with him twirling me in circles causing my stomach to lurch. Noticing my discomfort, he stopped abruptly and sat me back on the bench.

"We are having a child?"

"Yes, Gerald," I smiled, "we are having a child."

The happiness of the day was short lived when news from the King overshadowed the celebration we should have had.

"What is wrong?" I asked.

"I have received a message from the King. I will ride with my forces to meet Robert Belleme to secure Castle Bridgnorth. His brother, Robert the Duke of Normandy, is rumored to be back to occupy it."

"Why do you have to go?" I asked.

"Henry has many loyalists in the area, so it will simply be a diplomatic exercise ensuring peace. That is, if Belleme doesn't burn down a farm or two along the way," he said.

"What is wrong with him?"

"Belleme is a tyrant, he finds pleasure in the suffering of others. I've seen his face light up as a starving peasant's hand is removed for stealing an apple from his orchard." Henry shook his head, trying to rid his memory of such an atrocity.

"I remember Belleme from my time at Westminster, I've seen that very look on his face. King William had the same cruel nature and the two of them together would sometimes try to outdo the other. I don't miss those days under William's rule."

"Nor do I," Gerald said.

The next morning, the dust was still settling from the departure of my husband and the rest of his armored forces, when a royal standard and a small group of soldiers appeared through the castle gates led by King Henry I.

The ringing of the bell had brought us all to greet the unexpected royal visitors. I hadn't seen Henry since before his wedding day in Winchester, which seemed so long ago. Willa carried young Henry and placed him by my side but kept her hand in his so he wouldn't escape. He was young and needed to move about, but the commotion of the King's contingent kept him in awe and focused.

As soon as the King spotted the boy, without a second look at me dismounted from his horse throwing the reins back, assuming a groom close by would care for the beast. He instantly went down on one knee to face his son and smiled wide. I watched a wide grin appear on my son's face which seemed to please Henry.

"He is a fine boy," Henry said, looking up at me, the smile never leaving his face. He stood close, and I inhaled the familiar combination of sweat and leather. Memories I thought had been buried deep inconveniently resurfaced. I became conscious of my feet and kept them planted firmly on the earth. The same earth that my father had once ruled over and the same earth I now lived with my husband.

"Young Henry," he said, "do you know who I am?"

"Da Kin," he said.

"Yes Henry, I am the King, but I am also your father," he said.

"Papa?" My young son looked at me confused. My face flushed but Henry barely noticed the discretion.

"You look amazing," he said standing, grabbing my shoulders and kissing me full on the lips, not caring that his display was in full view of my ladies, Gerald's trusted guards, and my son. If anyone was shocked, they didn't show it. Henry was the King and everything in his land was his property, including me.

"I am sorry, my Lord. My husband is away at your bidding," I said, reminding him that because of him I was married.

Henry laughed. "Yes, that was carefully arranged so that I could avoid any awkwardness caused by an extended visit with my son."

"Your illegitimate son," I said before I could stop myself. Henry only smiled.

"Congratulations on the birth of a legitimate heir. I hear he is a healthy boy," I said quickly remining him that both our lives have continued. Edith had produced an heir and Henry's throne was secure.

"Will is a fine boy, already showing signs of becoming a leader." Henry said proudly. I wondered how an infant less than a year old could show leadership ability.

"I am fortunate with healthy sons," he said patting my boy on the head.

I had confirmed that Henry was also fortunate with a few daughters by other mistresses but decided not to mention it.

"We are enjoying the peace," I said hoping to change the subject from my boy.

"Peace is a wicked ally, my dear, too much makes you weak, not enough makes you weary," he said.

"Then it is that balance I hope will continue," I said.

"I have brought you a gift, my Lady." Henry signaled the carriage that was being held at the rear. An attendant opened the door and to my surprise, Brigit appeared. She ran to me and we embraced until both our eyes were full of tears.

"You are a welcome sight, my dear," I said brushing a tear that had escaped.

"As are you, my Lady," she said with a deep curtsey.

"Can I stay?" she asked. I had forgotten how red her hair was and how blue were those eyes. She really was quite stunning. It was her manners that were always lacking, and I never could figure out how to correct that.

"No one will take you from me again. I promise. I have missed you so much," I said. Remembering Henry, I turned to him, "Can she stay?"

"Please. If you don't take her, I was instructed to toss her in the river before returning to Westminster," he said.

"Jealous ladies?" I asked.

"Ha!" He laughed aloud. "The priest."

"Very funny, my King," Brigit said, as she grabbed me by the arm and leaned into me.

"I'm not jesting." He looked at me. "Good luck."

Brigit whispered in my ear, "The Queen is again with child, and she preferred I was not an available diversion for our King."

I felt a pang of jealousy but wasn't sure if it was the expected child or that Brigit may have distracted Henry. Regardless, I had no right and quickly swallowed any concern that might show in my expression.

"I thank God for her disapproval if it means I finally have you back," I whispered back.

For the next week, Henry spent every day entertaining our son with stories of exotic lands filled with strange animals. He presented him with cloaks lined with the same fur from those animals. He gave him a set of miniature soldiers carved out of wood from the New Forest, which caused our child to forget about the wooden sword Gerald had carved for him. He had even brought him a royal warhorse from his own stable, which was much too big for a toddler. I kept my displeasure to myself and pretended approval as Henry continued to bond with his son. Little Henry was quite taken with his father, which pleased Henry very much.

Every evening was a royal event complete with a King's feast featuring plenty of meats and wine. We were entertained with bards and troubadours that had been part of Henry's entourage. But every evening, as the festivities died down, Henry found his way to my chamber with no attempt to hide his intentions.

"You are the reason I am a married woman, and it is not proper that you visit my chamber so casually," I said the first evening he boldly entered my chambers and removed his robes exposing his nakedness.

"Princess, you are mine and I am yours. I married you to Gerald to keep you for myself. I never intended on staying away so long but my desire for you has not diminished. I think about you day and night."

"I am with child, my King."

"That is unfortunate. I might like to put my seed in you for another heir," he said with a wide smile and he slid on top of me.

"Please," I said but Henry easily pushed my legs apart and

took my body as if I was his. I did not resist but submitted to him like I had so many times before. I found the familiarity in his body comforting somehow and enjoyed his movements as he knew my weaknesses and brought me to pleasure more than once.

Every evening after, I would repeat my weak objections and end up waking up in his arms, a traitor to my husband and once again a common mistress to a King.

I felt guilt, not only for my participation but also because I enjoyed being with Henry in my bed. It brought back memories of my hopes and dreams as he whispered ideas in my head. Ideas that I had believed at one time, but no longer could.

I was ashamed of my weakness and disloyalty to Gerald, but what choice did I have? When Henry finally left Pembroke, he took my pride but left my heart. I held my son tight as he waved goodbye to his father.

When I was sure Henry was far enough away, I handed my son to Brigit and ran to my chamber, closed the door, and buried my head in the pillow. I cried for my son, I cried for my husband, and I cried for my unborn child. I didn't belong to any of them. I was the property of the King.

When Gerald returned, he didn't ask about the King's visit, but from the look on my face he knew. He put his arms around me, but I could feel disappointment in his hesitation. Where I felt shame, he felt humiliation. Henry had broken into our marriage and stayed there as a silent intruder.

It was the birth of our son and Henry's prolonged absence that seemed to repair the damage to our relationship. It was a joyous event and Gerald couldn't have been prouder of his first-born, a healthy baby boy we named William and just a year later we also welcomed a second son, Maurice, another healthy baby boy. I was once again happy and content busy looking after my husband and three young sons.

Gerald had been born at Windsor Castle and was a proud man from a prominent family, always a loyal servant since William the Conqueror. His marriage to me was ordered by the King and he obeyed the King's wishes, but he was never ordered to love me, but he did and in the beginning, those feelings were strong so when Henry once again sent Gerald on various minor campaigns or to settle simple land disputes that could have been settled by a lesser man, Gerald was further humiliated as Henry continued to invade our home with his music and wine. But even after the linens were laundered, fresh straw spread on the floors, and the castles doors opened wide, the smell of Henry remained.

The humiliation was too great, and it took a toll on our marriage. Every time he returned, he was a little more distant and rarely came to my chamber. I didn't know how to regain his love, and it was a lonely time for me, so I relied more and more on Brigit for companionship.

"I don't know why you tolerate that girl. She acts like she is the mistress here, ordering servants around like she isn't one," Gerald said to me on one of the rare occasions he sat with me at dinner.

"She has been a friend for a long time," I said, "she really is harmless."

"She is not your friend and I fear you place too much trust in her. Hear me now, someday she will betray you. She is loyal only to herself," he said between bites.

"Your words match my mother's the day I brought her home, but so far she has stayed true so I will give her that," I said.

"I do have some good news," Gerald said his face brightened, "Henry has approved our plans to build Carew in Deheubarth."

"That is great news," I said putting my arms around him. But he didn't return the gesture and actually shrugged me off burning a hole in my chest.

My husband's rejection hurt but I found happiness in my daily activities with my children and now planning our new home in Deheubarth. I decided to bring tutors into the castle instead of sending my boys away for their education. I wanted to keep an eye on what was poured into their minds. I would make sure they were taught Welsh history as well as the traditional education required by the Normans.

During one of King Henry's visits, my worst nightmare was realized.

"I think Henry should be educated in Windsor Castle with his brother and sister," he said.

"Henry, please," I said," don't take my son from me."

"I'm not taking him from you," he said. "You can visit any time and he can come visit you often."

"Henry, please," I said now letting the tears fall. "I have never asked you for anything, please don't take my son."

"It's settled, he will be educated in Windsor. It is for his own good, would you deny him the best education in the land?"

"Couldn't you send the books here so he can have his mother?"

"I have made my decision and he will have his father."

I couldn't take it any longer and ran to the yard where the boys were playing. I watched little Henry, only five years old. He was a bright boy with a brave heart and a kind spirit. He was charismatic like his father, and everyone loved him.

I was sick with grief as I watched my son happily wave as he was carted away to England.

"It's only a day and a half ride and we will visit often," Brigit said to me as she squeezed my hand tight. I was again heavy with child and did not want to pass my feelings on to the unborn baby, so I smiled and focused on the things that brought me joy in my life.

"You are right, I am overreacting. At least I know where he is, and Henry is granting me unlimited access. It could be worse."

I think Gerald was as upset as I was losing our boy. It wasn't until the birth of our third child, another son we named David, that Gerald's spirits lifted again and to his relief resembled his other sons. It seemed like my loving husband returned when we moved into our new home, Carew. It was as if we left all the negative memories behind Pembroke's walls.

CHAPTER 14

The Christmas Eisteddfod in my mother's birthplace of Powys promised to be the grandest affair of the year. Powys would have been my home if my marriage to my cousin Owain had taken place but it had not, and my place was with Gerald. Powys was still a magical place that I could imagine my mother growing into womanhood in the thick of the Pines.

It had been a successful year filled with peaceful alliances, bountiful harvests, and healthy children, which attracted people from every corner of our country that for so many years was plagued with infighting and Norman invasion.

Our arrival was hardly noticed, as all the Welsh and Norman landowners were arriving in droves. As we made our way through the main hall, we saw bards standing on small tables reciting poetry and telling stories of beautiful maidens and brave knights to an audience gathered round. The sounds in the hall were a mixture of musicians tuning their instruments and excited chatter among guests already partaking of the celebratory wine.

Cadwygan, our host was Owain's father and my mother's second cousin. He noticed me and pushed through the crowd to greet us.

"Welcome, Sir Gerald and Princess Nesta. I am so glad you decided to attend," Cadwygan said leaning in and kissing my cheek.

"It appears that your invitations have all been accepted," Gerald said.

"I believe you are correct, Gerald, but I think some of the interest is the contest I announced," he said, "I advertised a court position as Head Minstrel for the winner."

"That should be interesting," I said.

"More than interesting," he said, "so many entertainers arrived, we ran out of sleeping quarters and had to put bales in the courtyard to accommodate the fellows."

"I believe the land and residence that come with the position was more attractive than the position," said a voice from behind me.

Both Gerald and I turned to greet the voice and I had to swallow my surprise. I was looking at a man who looked like what I imagined the arc angel Gabriel might look like. He had long blonde hair curled in perfect rows, a perfectly strait nose, but it was his piercing blue eyes that struck me silent.

"My Lord, Gerald of Pembroke, may I present my son, Owain," Cadwygan said.

"My pleasure," he said with a bow of his head to Gerald and then turned to me, "and this must be the beautiful Nesta, Princess of Deheubarth, my once betrothed." He took my hand and kissed the top causing my face to turn hot.

It was Gerald's voice that finally broke the spell, "We are both at your service, my Lord."

I felt hot with guilt as I looked at my husband. I had previously confessed my long-ago betrothal to my cousin so this announcement didn't surprise him but the way Owain was looking at me must have made him uncomfortable.

"I admit I am looking forward to the entertainment," Gerald said.

"That's wonderful," Cadwygan said, "I would like to invite you to be one of the judges in my contest. You will have a front-row seat for the entertainment, and your fellow judges are other statesman of your rank and prestige."

"It would be my honor," Gerald said unenthusiastically, "but I couldn't leave my wife unattended all night."

"I will care for my cousin," Owain volunteered, causing my husband to roll his eyes. I could tell he had no interest in judging but knew a refusal would offend our host. I watched as he was led away to the join his fellow judges and I was left in the care of Owain.

"Come," he said putting his arm out for me to take hold. I felt like a young girl unsure of herself instead of the confident woman I had become.

He led me up the large wide staircase to the second floor where there was a door that led outside to a small porch that overlooked the entire courtyard where we could witness the activities below. The air was damp but not as cold as it usually was in December. I even considered removing my wrap, but it would expose more than I was willing in this private moment.

"How is it, cousin, that we haven't met before this day?" I asked to break up the awkwardness of the moment.

"Our country's unrest had caused me to find refuge in Ireland for my youth. The death of your father canceled the betrothal so there was never a reason to meet."

"You were in Ireland?"

"Yes."

"Do you know my brother, Gruffydd?"

"Of course, I know Gruffydd. We are good friends and allies. Your brother is a fierce warrior."

"So, he is well. That is a relief," I said careful not to expose my eagerness for such information.

"He plans on coming back and reclaim his birthright," Owain said.

"Can you get a message to him?" I asked now that Owain seemed to understand the situation.

"I can," he said, "before you leave here, pass it to me and I will make sure he receives it."

"Oh dear, thank you so much. It means everything to me," I said turning to the rail, looking out on the crowd below.

"I must confess, Nesta. I have heard rumors of your beauty and grace, but in this moment, I realize there are no words to describe the woman standing in front of me." His words were whispered in my ear as he stood behind me. He leaned in just enough that I could feel the light touch of his hip and smell the wild in the fur vest he wore. For a moment, I was lost in his presence that felt like a paralyzing protective cloak, causing panic in my chest, but also felt like I was a five-year-old wrapped in my father's arms.

"Sir, I am at a disadvantage. I have no words," I said softly.

"It doesn't matter the words, my Lady, only that you speak so that I can imagine the beautiful music that was lost to me these many years."

"Sir, as much as they flatter me, your words endanger my morality. I lack the freedom to return such romantic gestures." I turned now to face him, determined not to get lost in his control.

"If loyalty holds you back, know that I am aware of your affiliations to the King and his Norman Lord who keeps you on your own father's land. You do not belong to these foreigners. You belong to your people and have an obligation to them above a forced marriage."

The Welsh pride I had tamped down for so many years began to well up as he spoke, but I felt too entrenched in my current life to change. I was no longer a young woman born to a tribe where women were equal to men and wielded swords against their enemies.

"I admit an attraction to a life unlived. Whether your words are convincing or the longing for my childhood destiny has rekindled, my obligation to my heritage no longer involves my deeds. It will be the influence of my children becoming warriors who will stand with my brother when he returns."

"When your brother returns, he will need an alliance," he said.

"The alliance we were to provide with our marriage?"

"Exactly," he said smiling.

"Sir, you must forgive me, but my feet are weary, and I would like to retire."

"Please," Owain moved aside letting me pass, "I can lead you to your chamber for the night." We walked in silence, but I could feel the tension that had built between us. He stopped in front of the door and let me enter without interference.

"Until tomorrow," he said. I quickly entered and closed the door behind me. Our trunk was already in the room, but I didn't even bother to open it and simply removed my gown and slipped into the bed with my day shift. I had barely pulled the furs to my chin when Gerald entered the chamber, removed his clothes and slid in beside me.

Throughout the weekend, Owain found every opportunity to be next to me. He whispered of conspiracy into my ear, not always out of my husband's notice. It occurred to me that my husband may had been expertly engaged in the contest judging to allow Owain the opportunity.

The last evening was the final competition, complete with a King's feast. The guests were finding their seats when Owain and his entourage entered the dining hall. He liked to be the center of attention and refused to conform to convention. He was a powerful force with a charismatic personality. I kept my eyes on him as much as possible without making it obvious. He finally took his seat next to his father. The entertainers waited for him to be seated before beginning.

The bard called Otto was the first of the three finalists. He was a funny looking man with huge ears that stuck out from under white wisps of hair. His shoes were made of multicolored felt and sewn into tight points like the cap he wore on his head. His cloak was also made of felt that had been expertly embroidered with gold-threaded leaves covering the edges as if it were a royal cloak. His belly protruded as far out as a pregnant woman in her ninth month. His mouth was wide and his teeth large. I expected a small voice that matched his short stature but when he spoke, his voice was deep and loud. It easily reached the entire room and commanded our full attention.

"Ladies and Gentlemen, may I bring your attention to our host, Prince Cadwygan, who has brought us together this eve to celebrate with each other. Tonight, we leave our arms at the door and our neighbors are our friends." He grabbed a mug from a nearby table before jumping onto the small stage set up in the center of the room. "Long live Prince Cadwygan!"

The crowd roared and repeated Otto's words. "Long live Prince Cadwygan!"

"But he who provides this food and drink has provided us with something even better." He looked around the room pointing into the crowd until his crooked finger landed on Owain. "He has provided us a hero!" The crowd cheered loudly as Owain's smile widened at the attention directed toward him. Our eyes met for only a moment, but the moment was too long to avoid my husband's notice. Then Otto's loud voice again commanded our undivided attention.

> Regaining the land of Arwystli between Severn and Wye,
> A hero I say, a hero, say I,
> The sky turned dark and it began to rain,
> The knights they cheered, Owain! Owain!
> The Normans, the English, they shake in their boots,
> Not enough strong to overcome Welsh roots,
> Establishing control to Mechain and Cedewain.
> The King he acknowledges, Owain! Owain!
> Now to complete its Cantfeti,
> The land is safe in the hands of Powys,
> The men were fierce and the maidens not plain.
> The fine ladies, they sing, Owain! Owain!
> Drinking their ale and spilling their wine,
> No fear of rebellion, not even a sign,
> Once again in history, the right doest reign,
> The peasants they cheered, Owain! Owain!

Otto again turned with his arm outstretched, pointing to the crowd. "I said," he yelled, "the crowd they cheer—"

"Owain, Owain!" the guests repeated in thunderous explosion. Cadwygan patted his son Owain, acknowledging him as the protector of his land.

The next act featured a magician dressed in a black cloak complete with a hood he removed to show a long, crooked nose and long black hair. He looked like a raven transformed into a human. He silently pulled a white silk scarf from his neck and shook it, turning it this way and that to show the audience every angle. He balled it up in both hands. He shook it several times before unraveling it to release a white dove that flew over our heads.

Unfortunately, a magician could not be chosen as a minstrel. Any house who employed one would attract suspicion from the church. The people of Wales still clung to some of their ancient beliefs and were much more tolerant, but as more cathedrals littered the countryside, the more hangings for such actions. The church requires the magician to repeat the trick in front of the Bishop except in this case, exposing the secrets.

Ansyl, a wandering minstrel from the mountains, was the final competitor. He was a very thin young man with no hair on his face. He was dressed in a colorful tunic, simple black leather boots, and yellow leggings. I instantly recognized Ansyl. He was one of the young men who had served as an attendant to King William and been dismissed by Henry after William had been killed.

Ansyl stepped up onto the stage. He carried a small harp tucked under his arm and when he reached the center of the stage, he plucked a few notes to quiet the crowd. He then spun around so that his cape spread out, showing beautiful colors like that of a peacock in full display. His voice was loud and clear, and he did not need to raise it to be heard throughout the hall.

> Born in this land as daughter of Rhys,
> I witnessed her beauty, with mine own eyes,
> Her beauty so rare, there is no compare,
> Both inside and out, there's never a doubt,
> Valhalla, she begs for the blessings of Christ,
> Between England and Wales her loyalty sliced,
> A pawn of the King and wife of a knight,
> Our future depends on the end of her plight.

I was in shock and instantly looked to my husband. He had a blank look on his face as the crowd cheered. I felt my face flush as Ansyl bowed toward me before he turned to Cadwygan and then to the judges.

I took a walk along the Irish Sea to calm my upset mind. I could hear the commotion of the evening dying down in the distance. I longed for my home and the daily activities of my children to restore my sense of reality. But my thoughts were interrupted by Owain once again invading my space.

"Are you lost?" he asked.

"Hardly. The path is well lit by a clear sky, and the lights of the castle are a suitable guide to my destination," I said.

"Please forgive me," he said placing his body in my path. "You must understand my intentions."

"I understand fully," I said. "I cannot afford to live in your fantasy. I have made a commitment in front of God and will fulfill that obligation for as long as God demands it."

"I believe our destinies were set by God at our birth. It was not God who altered that path, but the actions of a selfish King who sent your father into a trap that changed your destiny and mine," he said.

"You are mistaken," I said. "It was my own lust that caused my destiny to change. I made selfish choices that have cost me my family and my people. I have to live with those choices, even if my heart says otherwise."

"You have an opportunity to make it right," he said excitedly.

"What are you tempting me with, Owain?"

"Run away with me," he said.

I laughed out loud. "I will never run away with you."

"Then I shall kidnap you," he said.

"Then my choice has been made for me," I said sarcastically.

I moved to walk around him when he grabbed my shoulders and kissed me softly on the lips. I wanted to resist but the softness of his lips combined with his warm breath kept me in his embrace. I felt as if there was a force stronger than my will holding me. I surrendered to him. I let passion and desire take me to a place I hadn't been in many years. These were feelings kept hidden since the first kiss with Henry. The child that lived in that kiss had been replaced by a woman full of life experience, anger, regret, and duty. For that moment, I let go and gave myself to this beautiful man in the middle of a small patch of Welsh grass. My passion had been pent up for so long it seemed to explode when released.

"Now you are mine," Owain whispered.

CHAPTER 15

Over the next few months, Owain and his retinue found reasons to pass through Deheubarth often, and each time we would find an opportunity to be alone and explore the passion we had for one another. It was like a fine wine served on the holiest of days when you are only allowed one cup. The taste is wonderful, but it isn't enough to completely quench your thirst.

Owain never stopped his requests for me to return to Powys with him and I refused each time. While I did enjoy his company, I could not leave my three sons.

It was the last day of the month when the moon was no longer full. I had a strange feeling at the nape of my neck. The air was typically thick. The rain-soaked earth found relief as the sun's warm rays coaxed the daffodil bulbs from hibernation just in time for Saint David's Day. I was restless, aware that familiar night sounds seemed absent. We had moved to Carew Castle only a short time ago, so only half our household had been set up. We would move the remaining furnishings in the next few weeks as the roads hardened and eased the travel of the loaded carts.

In the darkest part of that night, I woke. I put a wool shawl around my shoulders and laid enough oak on the fire to last until morning. Gerald was dead to the world except for the occasional snort which didn't bother me. A small glow caught my attention as I passed the window. I moved closer looking out to the courtyard where I caught sight of two soldiers carrying torches and touching them to our newly built wooden structures.

"Where are our guards?" I said loudly, "Gerald, we are under siege."

Gerald flew from the bed and was fully dressed before I could say anything more. "Stay here," he told me. I looked out the window again and that is when I saw him. Owain was the invader.

"Gerald," I called as I ran out of the room and caught him before he had armed himself. "It is Owain."

"Owain?" he asked.

"He and his men, I'm sure," I said.

"How can you be so sure?" he asked.

"He mentioned it when he asked me to voluntarily go with him. When I refused, he made it a threat. Your life, I am afraid, is in danger. He knows our layout and if you are dead, he can claim me." I watched Gerald's expression change quickly from confusion to anger. I knew he was suspicious that this might have been my plan, too. "This is not my plan. I will never forgive him for his actions tonight. My fear now is for your life," I said.

Gerald touched the sword that he had just fastened securely to his side. "I will have my revenge."

"My love, please," I said. "We must save your life for our children's future."

"I am not running away and leaving you here to fend for yourself," he said.

"I am begging you. You know he will not harm me, and I need you to survive to care for our children." I grabbed Gerald's arm and led him to the privy closet. "This is the only way out," I said, opening the closet door and pointing to the hole.

"I am not going to hide in there," Gerald said.

"You won't be hiding," I said. "You must slide through."

"It's a shit hole, Nesta."

"There is no other option. It's the only escape. It's not like it's been in use for very long. Imagine it a year from now," I said.

"It's still shit, no matter the amount," he said, but hearing the commotion in our halls, he surprisingly climbed into the trough that would deliver him to the moat below. From there, he would be able to swim to the canal. I closed the privy door and quickly left my room, hoping Gerald's escape wouldn't be discovered. As I approached the staircase, Owain was already on his way up, taking two steps as one.

"Where is your husband?" he asked with a determined look on his face.

"I don't know," I said. "Why are you doing this?"

"You are mine."

"I am married."

"You will soon be widowed," he said loudly, as he brushed past me, opening and closing doors down the hall.

"Please stop, Owain. You will scare the children," I pleaded.

He stopped and came back to where I stood guarded by one of his men. "I can no longer live without you," he said, grabbing me around the waist. He pulled me to him and forced a kiss that I did not resist.

"You came to kill my husband?" I asked, when I got my breath back.

"I see no other option," he said.

"If you harm my husband or my children, you must also kill me, because I will never forgive you," I said.

"Tonight, settles a dispute with the past, and will set things right," he said.

"If you are so desperate for my company, then take me peacefully. Leave my children to their father's care," I said as I put my hands on his cheeks so he would focus on my face instead of wildly looking around. "I will come willingly, but we must go now. We can make a clean escape. Gerald is not here and there is no reason to stay longer."

"Okay, but we will have to take the children," he said.

"We leave the children, or I will resist. You may have my body but not my soul. I promise only that." I moved my hands from his face and put one in his hand. I could tell Owain was weighing his options. He chose to take me willingly. I watched his resolve as he pulled me down the stairs one at a time until we reached the door, where he dropped my hand and moved back to the stairs with his hand on the hilt of his sword.

"We must go," I said, walking out the door. To my relief, Owain followed. I didn't dare look toward the moat in fear of revealing Gerald's escape route, and rekindling Owain's desire to kill him. I simply looked ahead to an uncertain future, not sure what emotion to bring along.

I looked for Brigit who I knew would be close and spotted her as I mounted the steed brought to me by one of Owain's men.

"Take care of the children," I said. "I will send word as soon as I can."

She shook her head and moved back letting the horses gather and out the gate with no resistance.

Owain handed me a cloak that I wrapped around me.

"It's going to be a long night," he said. "We have to put as much distance as we can before daylight."

"He won't follow us, I'm sure," I said.

"Then he is a fool," Owain said.

For the next few days, we traveled along the coast only stopping to rest late at night under the cover of the thick forest until we reached hills covered in blue and white rock. I imagined this is where great dragons lived, perching high on the crags looking into the valley covered in a sea of blue heather.

We finally reached our destination. It was a small castle that was built and abandoned by the Romans who built it as a fortress, protected on three sides by the mountainous terrain of the Boncan Dinas, protecting it from the rear and two sides and the vast sand and pebble beach of the Cardigan Bay made it impossible to reach when it was high tide. It was set very close to the sea so the floodgates could only be opened when the tide was low to allow entrance. There was no way they would be discovered.

"How did you find such a place?" I asked.

"It is a secret place known only to a small number of people in my family. We discovered it a generation ago and use it rarely," he said.

"I worry that my children will suffer the loss of their mother," I said wearily.

"They are safe," he assured me.

I smiled bravely at my capture, unsure of the future. Owain sat so proud as if he had won another great battle against the Norman forces in rescuing a Welsh Princess, but this Welsh Princess spent half her life under Norman care and was accustomed to the Anglo-Norman lifestyle.

"Will you ask for a ransom?" I asked Owain teasingly.

"I have exactly what I want. Are you not pleased to be free from the Normans?" Owain stopped to look me straight in the eye.

He put his hand on my cheek. "I am sorry," he said, "but you are under my care now and there is nothing you could wish for that I will not do everything in my power to provide. I understand the loss of your children is a pull on your heart but if it becomes too unbearable, we can send for them."

I couldn't imagine my children being stolen from their father or asking them to endure the isolation of this place. It would be unfair to expect them to suffer for my selfish motivations.

"You are going to love it here," Owain took my hand and kissed the back of it. "We are going to be very happy."

How did this all happen? What would I do each day? I watched the floodgates close behind us, sealing us in behind a wall of sea.

"As long as those gates are closed, the water will never come up as far as the castle, "Owain said, interpreting the worry on my face to the threat of flood.

"But what if the gates are left open?" I asked.

"That can never happen. See that man over there?" He pointed to the old man that was working on securing the long wooden posts back into place. "It is his only task to keep the gate secured for the tide changes," he assured her. "He has been doing it since he took over the task from his own father many years ago."

"No one lives forever," I said.

"Then it is fortunate that he also has a son."

It was a relief to see that the castle had a full staff and it had some of the comforts I was used to. When I had first arrived, I imagined I might have to learn to grow a crop or milk a cow. Not that I didn't think I was capable, but I had no experience.

The household staff were very kind and seemed happy to have me as their lady. Most of them spoke the old Welsh language spoken in my childhood home causing me to miss my parents. It looked as though this castle had only been used as a military stronghold rather than a residence; there were no wall hangings, window coverings, or decoration of any kind. Many rooms were small and lacked furniture, and the furniture that did exist was rough and well worn.

Noticing my concern, Owain promised to refurbish the entire castle, starting with my rooms.

"As long as there is wood for the fire and honey for my bread, you will not suffer my complaints," I said. "I would like a change of clothing if possible." I had been riding for all this time in my sleeping shift wrapped in the fur coats Owain provided to me.

"I have a seamstress and a laundress at your service. My father is sending a few additional ladies for your service," he said.

"Your father is aware of your kidnapping of a wife and mother?" I asked.

"Are you implying you are not here at your own free will, my lady?" Owain said with a sly smile. "I admit the invitation was unconventional, but your lack of resistance was not a denial. If I didn't think your desire for my arms wasn't genuine, I wouldn't have given you a way out of your mundane existence."

"What is my existence now here, hidden from the world?"

I said.

"All things can change. Your brother is well prepared to take his place in your country as its rightful heir. Our forces are well trained and have held our own borders and will honor the alliances promised long ago," he said in a serious tone.

He took me in his arms and swung me around like a child. "It will be okay. I promise," he said playfully.

I smiled as bravely as I could as reality set in. I didn't belong here. I was a foreigner in my own country. Owain was a very handsome, powerful and sweet but he didn't know me like Gerald. He only knew the promise of me. I was suddenly overcome with longing for the innocence of childhood. I allowed Henry to steal my virgin heart, I submitted to Gerald under the contract of marriage, and now I was giving into an obsession with Owain at the cost of my freedom.

Owain brought me to him and held me tight. His body against mine had too much power against my will and I easily yielded to him. I was not convinced to love him yet but the wanting of him was real and he stirred me like no other.

For the next few months, we slept in the same bed, not able to leave the warmth of the other. The raw passion was addictive and there was not a day we didn't sneak off outside the eyes of the household to explore the body of the other. I admit that it was equal desire, and neither could get enough.

Before too long, this unbridled passion caused me to loosen the ties of my gowns to expose a swollen belly. After missing two courses, I had to admit to Owain the child growing inside me. Owain was thrilled since this was his first child, but I had to remind him this child was a result of captivity and wouldn't be accepted as a legitimate heir since we were not legally married.

"The Welsh laws are not as clear as that," Owain told me. "We are betrothed, you were captured by the Normans and forced into a marriage. They have invaded not only our lands but also our bloodlines."

"But the marriage was blessed by God," I said.

"Their God, not our gods," he said. "But whoever's god, once Gerald is dead, you will marry the man you were betrothed to."

CHAPTER 16

As the child pushed on my ribs and moved about in my belly, I worried about the sons I left behind, growing into men with no influence of their Welsh mother. I secretly wished the child I carried was a girl so that I could easily take her when I returned. A Welsh boy, legitimate or not, of two royal houses would pose a threat to the Normans and would never be safe. I believe even Gerald would sacrifice a child born of two Welsh houses. As these thoughts ran through my head, I realized that I was looking at my situation as temporary.

"I think we need a midwife," I told Owain.

Panic arose on his face, "Now?"

"No, not now but this is not my first child, and it could be any time before the season changes. Because of our remote location, it would be safe to have her near," I said.

"I'll send someone tomorrow," he said.

"I do not trust your representative. I need to choose the right one. I will go to the village with you," I told him, crossing my arms to show I wouldn't be dissuaded.

The next morning, soon after we broke fast, I donned a plain long cloak with a full hood to disguise my identity. Owain assigned me only one man who would pose as a companion rather than an armed guard to avoid suspicion in such a small village.

Owain and his men stayed far enough behind to not appear as we were traveling together but close enough to provide aid if necessary. My stomach was swelled more than any of my other children and I did not look forward to the birth. Robert, my firstborn, was the hardest delivery but I was so young, I recovered quickly. But with each one after, it took a little longer to return to normal.

As we reached the edge of the village, I could see groups of thatched roofs emitting smoke from the holes in the sides. It reminded me of my youth when I had the luxury of time and could let my imagination run. I imagined the smoke as giant snakes escaping through the thatched roofs becoming other magical creatures before they disappeared into the sky only to concentrate far above our heads into the clouds.

This small village was almost identical to many of the small villages scattered across Wales. Most were not actual shops, but roughly constructed booths of thin logs held together with twine and twisted roots that supported the thatched roofs. It was the familiar smells of freshly baked bread and meat pies that reached my nose first reminding me of times past. I breathed in deeply, recognizing a hunger that rarely left me during this pregnancy. I adjusted my hood as the number of travelers increased when we turned onto the main road of the town.

The ride was also more exhausting than it should have been so it was a great relief when we finally reached the abbey where I could rest and safely interview potential midwives.

Because we were deep into Welsh country where the Normans hadn't yet invaded, the nuns who ran this particular abbey were loyal to their Welsh ancestors and still secretly practiced some of the old ways.

"Welcome, child," an older nun greeted me with both hands around mine. "Please sit and rest," motioning to a large chair in front of the hearth that was already heating my face. She took my cloak and I sat. She reached behind her where another younger nun held a tray. She handed me a cup of spiced apple ale and a piece of sweet bread.

"Thank you, sister," I said sipping the ale. "I hope I don't fall asleep before the first woman arrives."

"We expected you a while ago, so the candidates are already waiting. Whenever you are ready, we may begin the interviews," she said.

"I am afraid the journey took longer as I had to rest often," I placed my hand on my stomach. "This one is sure to have a strong will as he already dictates my life. But of course, we can begin." I took another sip of the ale and several bites of the sweet roll which melted in my mouth.

The younger nun that was holding the tray earlier was now holding a large screen along with another young nun and placed it before me.

"In order to keep your identity confidential," the older nun explained.

"I understand, and thank you for all the trouble," I said.

I ate the remainder of the roll and finished the ale, wishing for another while the first candidate was seated on the other side of the screen.

"Thank you for meeting in such an unusual manner," I said when I was sure she was settled. "Can you tell me a little about yourself?"

"I am Mariam from the wood. My own mother died when I was a child, so I raised four younger sisters until my father disappeared and we were fostered apart. I was fortunate to be welcomed by a widow who shared her knowledge of the wood and I learned the old ways in herbal healing."

"Have you any experience as a midwife?" I asked.

"I've seen it done many times by my foster mother, but I have only delivered one child, my Lady," she said, "but it is such a natural thing, most of the work is done by the mother. It's the dealing with everything after that is important."

"This isn't my first child," I said.

"Then you know full well," she said.

"I do," I said.

"You may go," the older nun told the woman as she came from behind the screen and handed me another cup of ale.

Mariam walked out as Owain barged past her moving the screen aside. Mariam looked back and met my eye. I smiled at her and she smiled back. I liked her. I knew she was the one I would choose but there were several others waiting.

"Have you settled on a midwife?" he asked.

"We have two more," the sisters said.

"We don't have all day," he said, "which one do you recommend sister?"

"I would recommend—"

"I choose Mariam," I said interrupting the nun.

"She is the least experienced," the nun said. "That is why I put her first. I wouldn't have even brought her in except we could only locate two others in such short notice."

"I choose Mariam," I said again.

"So, it is settled, Sister. Please fetch Mariam and send her to the Barron's home," Owain said, fishing out some silver and handing it to the senior nun. "I thank you for your help and especially for your discretion." Her hand was still extended, and he delivered another piece of silver, seemingly satisfying her as she closed her boney fingers around it.

"Bless you both," she said, moving aside to let us pass.

Soon we were outside and safely out of the range to be overheard.

"There is trouble here. I have information that there have been inquiries,"

"By whom?" I asked.

"The King."

"Henry?"

"My uncle has been offered a rich reward for your location. He said the reward is so great, villagers are forming alliances to find you."

"How does he know I am here?"

"It's not just local, the delegation formed to recover you spans the entire country. It seems the King is desperate for your return and has made a statement of war against any who holds you. His man, Hait, Sheriff of Pembroke, is the man in charge."

"It's always Hait," I said out loud to myself.

"Supporters are leaving false clues leading the delegates

to dead ends. I'm not sure how long this ploy will be affective. My uncle is here somewhere looking for us. Your husband must be an important Knight in his service to go to such an extent to locate and return his wife," he said.

I kept silent. I knew the truth—it was Henry who desired me within his reach. Henry had no concern for Gerald or my children except they were the means to keep me under his control and at his disposal.

"Do I have a chance to get a few things?" I asked Owain.

"As long as you stay on the main street and don't speak to anyone unnecessarily. I am going to attempt to locate my uncle, Iorweth."

Keeping my hood low, I walked through the village, leaving my gelding with my guard at the end of the road. I found a vendor with simple cloth and picked out several pieces for the nursery. I was enjoying the freedom away from the constant attendants looking after me or making sure I didn't escape, so I walked slowly along the shops.

It was getting late and many of the vendors were packing up their wares onto handcarts and were heading toward their homes for the evening. I looked back and saw my companion was out of sight, but I had no place to go. I was resigned to live with Owain until the day I was discovered, which I felt was growing near, for when Henry is determined, no one can stop him from getting his wishes.

That is when I saw out of the corner of my eye an old woman come across the street toward me. I quickly turned to avoid her path, but she was speaking old Welsh.

"Please help," she said.

I tried to turn away, but she moved into my path. "Please help," she repeated, "my daughter, she is..."

I couldn't make out the last part, but she pulled me back to the shop across the street from where she first appeared.

We entered what appeared to be a candle shop. The sweet smell of beeswax permeated the air and there were various stages of wax-covered wicks hanging from braided vines across the room. There were also dried plants hanging in bundles tied and hung upside down. There was barely enough room to walk upright, but the woman continued to pull me through the small room to the back to where a woman was lying on a bed of straw in the middle.

I leaned down to her and saw she was a young woman, white-faced and sweaty. Her eyes were closed and unresponsive. I brought my face to hers to hear her breath as shallow. That's when I noticed, she was heavily pregnant.

"She is dying," I said to the old woman who stood over us, staring with her watery eyes.

"Yes," she said in her thick Welsh accent. "Please help her."

"What am I supposed to do?" I asked the woman.

"Save the child," she said. I lifted the thin blanket that had been draped across the girl and saw a pool of blood between her legs, but it was the small foot I touched that concerned me. I had heard of this type of birth, but I was not a midwife, and I wasn't sure what to do until my instincts took over and I reached in to locate the other foot and together pulled the child from its dying mother. It was a girl. I held her upside down until she cried. I found a knife sitting on a small shelf and cut the umbilical cord from its mother. I tied it a knot to stop the blood and took the thin blanket and swaddled her.

"Hello," I called out several times. The old woman had disappeared, and I was here alone with a dying woman and a baby who was probably going to die if I didn't do something.

I said a silent prayer, but it was no use; the young woman took her final breath in a deep gasp and I felt the coldness of the room overtake us. I held the child close as I left her mother's shell unattended.

I looked outside the shop for the old woman. She was nowhere in sight. It was getting dark and the street was silent. Where had she gone? "I can't possibly take this child," I said out loud to the dark empty street.

But I looked at the small baby girl in my arms. I have never experienced the love of a daughter and I was about to have another child very soon. The tiny thing mewed like a small kitten, too weak to cry but the sound could bring attention to me so to quiet her, I slipped her under my cloak, exposed my breast to her and surprisingly she latched on easily. The suckling was painful as my nipples were not ready to receive a child, but it seemed to satisfy her. If I had not already had several children, it would have been impossible but soon the milk flowed freely, and the child fell asleep.

The large figure of Owain was soon moving toward me causing me to feel some relief.

"Where have you been?" he said, obviously irritated with me.

I exposed the child's head who was still latched to my aching breast. He became more confused as he touched my still swollen belly. I pointed to the shop and he entered. A few minutes later, he came out shaking his head and looked around making sure no one saw us.

"Leave it here," he said.

"She is an orphan. We can't leave her here to die," I said. I wasn't sure if it was the look on my face or his determination to get off the street, but he whistled to the guard who brought the horses.

"What are we going to do with this child?" he asked as he rode close to me.

"We will bring her with us," I said.

"We will leave her with the nuns," he said, "but we are definitely not bringing a child with us." He paused before adding, "Is that blood on your cloak?"

I looked down and saw a large stain of blood covering a large section of my cloak. "Turn it inside out," he told me. "Quickly."

He looked around and we were still alone, and I struggled to comply. With one arm balancing the child, I kept silent as I didn't want to upset him, and he didn't ask any questions.

As soon as we reached the Barron's dwelling, I found Mariam and handed her the child.

"I am not sure she will live," I said.

Mariam took the child from my arms and set her down, opened the blanket and examined each toe and finger. I noticed a red marking on her upper thigh and pointed to it. "It's just a birthmark, she is well underweight but seems healthy enough," she said.

"Shall we call her Angaret?" I asked.

"A gift from God," Mariam said, "I think it is a wonderful name."

"We need a wet nurse," I said.

"I know of a woman," Mariam said.

"Send for her quickly," I said.

"We are not taking the child," Owain said overhearing our conversation.

"Please, Owain," I said, "if we turn her over to the nuns, it may draw attention to them and it may slip that we had just been to the abbey."

"A dead girl in a candlemaker's hut surely won't create any attention," he said.

"But no one could tie us to that location," I said.

"Fine, tell the guard where to find the wet nurse and have them meet us at the gate at the sea entrance by tomorrow morning. We need to keep our caravan small as we travel. You must keep the child out of sight. Do you understand?" He looked at Mariam and me, and we both nodded our heads.

We left before sunrise in order to leave the village unnoticed. It was a slow ride as my aching back could only take so much, causing us to stop often so I could get off the horse to rest. When we took a break at noon, I took the child, nursed her while Mariam found some nettles and other ingredients from the forest floor. She stirred the mixture together and tore a generous piece of cloth from her undergarment, packed it, and tied warm compress around my waist, leaving the pack on my back creating instant relief.

"This will last a few hours," she said reaching for the child.

Owain helped me back on my horse and we continued

our travels. Unfortunately, all the delays caused us to miss the first tide, so it would be several hours waiting for the tide to recede enough to be able to enter the gates to the stronghold. As we watched the sun lower over the horizon, Iorweth, Owain's uncle, arrived. I recognized him right away since he was a twin in looks to his brother, Cadwygan, Owain's father.

The two men dismounted their horses and greeted each other with a stiff hug.

"What's the news, uncle?" Owain said.

"It's dire, I'm afraid," he said looking at the group gathered around. Owain nodded his head, indicating Iorweth's freedom to speak.

"Hait has arrived in Powys and has threatened your father with exile and confiscation of all his lands. Cadwygan has denied conspiracy with you, but Hait claims to have gathered information from weak countrymen who cannot resist the bribe."

"Desperate men will claim anything for silver," Owain said.

"Hait claims he has reputable sources," Iorweth said.

"What does my father say?" Owain asked.

"Your father's forces are weak and neighboring forces won't find anyone to convince to stand with him. He has sent me to convince you to release Nesta," he said. "I am sorry, my Lady." He looked toward me.

"We are about to have a child," Owain said, looking at me and them back to Iorweth. "Can we stall them?"

"How?" Iorweth asked. "Your father is going to lose his land; you will have nothing to return to."

"I don't care," he said.

"Say she is ill and cannot travel right away, but if we promise to return her by winter solstice, will they stay their siege?"

"Your father is not going to like this solution. He specifically said for me to deliver the Princess to him."

"Well, tell my father the situation. You cannot take her

across the country in this condition."

"Are you considering releasing me back to the English?" I asked Owain.

"No, but if I buy time, it will give us time to find a solution," Owain said.

"If you don't return her, Owain, you are sacrificing everything your ancestors won. Please consider the consequences."

Owain did not release me and only weeks later I delivered a son. Owain was a proud father and this boy was the largest child I had born. His lungs were healthy, and he made himself known.

A messenger soon arrived with the news that Cadwygan's lands were being distributed to the local barons and that Cadwygan had himself escaped but not before one of the landowners exposed the remote location in Gwynedd near the coast where I was being held.

"You need to escape," I told Owain.

"We will go to Ireland," he said.

"I cannot go. Henry will not stop; he will continue to search for me and destroy your family. If I go back willingly, it might not be too late to recover your father's lands," I said. "You cannot build allies with the King's men at your back."

"You are right," he said. "This is a turning point, but the Welsh cannot be defeated so easily. I will retreat for now and find strength overseas. But when I return, I will not only win my lands back but return yours as well."

"Will you enlist Gruffydd to your cause?" I asked.

"It is his cause, too. It is time our country is free again."

"I believe you," I said softly. He grabbed my waist and kissed me hard.

"I will release you, but you cannot take my son," he said.

"I know," I said. "Llywelyn and Angaret will never be safe with me."

I felt the tears well but didn't allow them to fall. I was tired of crying and vowed to use the heartache I felt to avenge my people. I was tired of feeling weak and out of control.

"I cannot bear to leave these children," I said, "my heart is broken."

"God is closest to those with broken hearts," Mariam said as she put her arms around me.

"They will remain safe here until I can return them to you. I promise with my life."

I held my son close and kissed his plump red cheeks and kissed my small girl on the head. I turned to Mariam, who was a second mother anyway.

"Take care of my babies," I said.

"Like they were my own," she said. Mariam would stay at the stronghold and claim the children as her own, she would be well-funded until Owain or I could arrange a closer situation. The church had not recorded either of the children's birth so there was no legal record of either birth or birthrights. I was confident they would remain safe.

CHAPTER 17

Owain successfully escaped on a ship sent earlier by his uncle before Hait had arrived. At first, the gatekeeper refused the King's men entry even at the risk of his own life until I sent word to allow them free access. There were at least a dozen men riding under the King's standard obviously expecting some resistance, but all they were greeted with was myself and our limited household staff.

Hait was the lead rider and stood tall in the saddle. He was wearing light chainmail and a full helmet with the face shield up so I could see his bright blue eyes when he spotted me. He jumped from his horse and ran toward me as I ran toward him.

"Once my capture, now my savior," I said.

"But the destination, the same," he said smiling.

"Are you taking me to the King?" I asked looking into his intense blue eyes.

"Those are my orders, my lady."

"What of my husband?"

"Gerald is well but busy settling the Welsh uprisings as a result of Henry confiscating the lands of Cadwygan. I am to deliver you to Westminster before you can return to Carew."

"Does Gerald know I have been found?"

"I honestly don't know but I also don't think so," Hait said watching my face but found no change in expression.

"I have been gone a long time," I said but didn't expect any response.

"And you have been missed," he said.

The stronghold was limited in supplies, but the household staff found enough to feed Hait's men and refresh the horses, giving me time to pack the few things I cared to bring back with me. I came with little and would leave with little.

As we rode over the next few days, Hait caught me up on all of the royal gossip but knew little of Gerald's activities.

When we finally arrived at Westminster, Henry wasn't there, but a message had been sent to Windsor that I had arrived. While I waited, I enjoyed the comforts of the castle. I took a long warm bath and lathered myself with soap made with lavender and mint. I plaited my hair using berry-stained ribbons and let the ladies dress me in silk and lace. I couldn't remember feeling so alive.

As I entered the dining hall, I was greeted with familiar faces, including Hait who was waiting near the entrance for me. He held his arm so I could weave mine through as he led me to my seat at the table.

"You look stunning," Hait said in my ear.

"I honestly feel like a new woman," I said as he then pulled a chair, allowing me to sit before he took his seat at the opposite end of the dining table.

Just as the first course of meats and cheeses was laid in front of me, the dining hall doors flew open as Henry rushed into the hall. Everyone stood to greet the King, but he ignored them all and made his way to me, grabbing my middle almost lifting me off my feet.

"Oh, my beautiful girl," he said almost singing, "you have been sorely missed." Henry kissed me full on the lips in front of an entire room full of guests, and I felt my face turn red.

"Your Grace," I said bowing my head slightly.

"Let me look at you." He turned me this way and that. "A little thin but that can be remedied." Henry's smile was broad, but I noticed a few lines at the corners of his eyes and around his mouth, his hair thinning on top, and that he was much heavier than before, which gave him a resemblance to his brother William.

"You look well, my Lord," I said.

"I'm a bit thicker," he said patting his middle. I smiled politely but then noticed the two young men that had accompanied him through the door. One of the boys was a thin replica of his mother, which I assumed was Henry's heir, Will, and the other boy taller than his father but a younger version of the same, my son Henry.

"Henry," I said putting my hand out to my son.

"Mother," he said in a voice I did not recognize for it was now a man's voice. He took my hand in his and bowed his head slightly.

"I have missed you so," I said.

"You have been missed," he said smiling.

"Your son is an accomplished swordsman and a master at the bow," King Henry said proudly.

"I would love to see a demonstration," I said.

"I have a hawk," he said proudly. I instantly thought of Gruffydd and how proud he was of his falcon. I so wished my brother could see his godson today.

"Tomorrow we shall have a demonstration," Henry said. "Tonight, we celebrate our lost Princess who has been found."

The next few days and nights were filled with wine and song. The celebration, although it was in my honor, was exhausting. I had gotten used to a quiet existence, so I was ready to go Welsh home and see my other three sons.

At night when Henry came to my chamber, I tolerated him but had no desire for him. Anything I had ever felt for him had disappeared years ago. I felt nothing for this man who used me as if I was his property.

While I was away, I feel like time stood still but here in court, it was obvious that life continued on. I couldn't wait to see my boys in Deheubarth and see the changes in them which I am sure will be as drastic as my son, Henry. I had left little boys and they were well on their way to grown men.

Hait volunteered to escort me home when Henry finally released me. It took two full days until we finally arrived well after the sun had set. The gate was opened and closed without much commotion as the guard recognized Hait as a regular visitor and didn't give me a second thought.

I was tired but wanted to face Gerald before I shut my eyes. My heart was unsure of how I would be received. Would he be excited or disappointed? I missed his gentle ways and the stability of him.

The corridor was still lit with the evening candles, so I stepped into his outer chamber. The door was slightly open, so I quietly slipped in. I could see the glow of the fire in the hearth of his privy chamber. I decided to just look upon him and not wake him but that is when I heard voices. It wasn't his voice; it was definitely a woman's tone. My heart sank but how could I blame him for keeping company while I was away. I should have given up and returned to my own chamber, but my curiosity was too strong, so I moved closer to the door and pushed it just a little wider. That is when I saw the flaming red hair of Brigit. I covered my mouth to stifle a gasp. She sat above him grunting like a freshly slopped hog.

"I know what you like," she said in between snorts and grunts.

"Shut up!" Gerald said in a harsh tone I had never heard from him. He pushed her off the top of him exposing his full erection. He sat up as he spun her around before forcing her face into the bed as he took a position behind her, forcing himself into her as she let out a deep moan. He moved a few times into her before he released with a final violent thrust. Again, I should have left but I stood frozen in disbelief. I had never watched anyone have sex much less these two people usually familiar to me now strangers.

"Now leave," Gerald said forcefully pointing to the very door where I stood hidden only by the shadow.

Brigit laughed. "Don't think I don't see how you desire me. You have never experienced a woman like me. I am the one who satisfies your every desire."

"You are nothing but a whore, Brigit. You climb into my bed hoping for your status to increase but you will never be anything more."

"Nesta will never satisfy your needs. You forget she willingly left your bed for her Welsh cousin. You were lucky to escape with your life." With her voice now soft, she added, "you deserve a woman who puts your needs above her own. I have served you well as months became years with no question. I know you have feelings for me." She knelt in front of him and placed a hand on his leg.

He pushed her hand away. "I have no feelings for you, and the only person you serve is yourself. Don't think because I stick my prick in you once in a while changes me into a dullard. I use you as I use a trencher when I'm hungry."

"You are a fool, Gerald," she said rising between his legs and moving her face close to him. But she tempted her fate with her words as he grabbed a fist full of her hair and threw her to the floor as she let out a screech.

"I said, get out," he said again loudly. "Just get out."

She slowly rose to her feet and found her linen night dress that she slipped over her head while Gerald settled into his bed pulling the furs to his chest. I couldn't see his face but would imagine the blankness of his stare. I moved further into the shadows until Brigit stomped her way past me out the door of the outer chamber. I stayed hidden until I could hear Gerald's deep breaths turn into a familiar rhythmic pattern.

I was a ghost floating quietly down the long hall as the candles sputtered with the last remnants of wax and wick, clinging to the metal hangers with just the slightest movement as I walked past, caused their extinction, leaving only darkness behind me.

When I reached my chambers, it was cold even though a full-flamed fire filled the hearth. The cool stone walls battled the new coals for space leaving me an unwelcome guest instead of the familiar inhabitant of the past.

Even my own mementos lining the dusty shelves seemed like old friends turned strangers from too much time passed. I shivered and struggled to loosen the ties that held me together.

Finally, free from its tethers, I let the heavy gown drop to the floor. I stepped out of the pile of silk and lace and crawled under the bedding furs. I disappeared from the world by slipping deep into the bed, covering my face and head. My toes still cold, I brought my knees to my chest like a child encased in a mother's womb. I was too exhausted to even cry so I just closed my eyes and let my dreams carry me into the world of my childhood, a world without worries.

I woke to a commotion and the most amazing smells as I wearily peeked out of the cocoon I had created. I saw the most wonderful sight I could imagine. It was the smiling face of Willa.

"Welcome back, my Lady," said Willa who was standing at the end of the bed with both hands on her wide hips. Her bosom looked like two giant goose down pillows stuffed into cases much too small. She signaled a younger woman from the door to place a tray full of sweet breads and a steaming pot of herbal tea. The aroma teased me out from under the warm furs, reminding my stomach how long it had been since I had eaten.

Hait had been strict in our travels the day before as he never stopped to cook so we survived on dried meats and watered ale on our two-day journey. I almost wished the bright full moon that had been bright enough to guide us the last few miles would have hidden itself behind winter clouds, allowing us enough delay to save my memory of the night before. I was so weary from travel; I considered the possibility of a bad dream until I heard her voice.

"Nesta, I can't believe you are home. We received word only yesterday that you were free from Owain's grips. I am so happy to have my dearest friend back," she said as she forced herself past Willa and sat on the edge of my bed. I noticed Willa move her eyes toward the ceiling and shook her head abandoning my side to stoke the fire.

"I'm surprised you are out of your own bed so early," I said noticing the once flawless white skin now dull and her nose reddened by too much wine. Hard lines surrounded her eyes and the corners of her mouth. Her bright blue eyes, once so full of sparkle, were now narrow and suspicious. I didn't recognize the woman that stood before me or maybe I actually saw her for the first time. I couldn't even pretend to be happy to see her, the disappointment too raw. The pity that once promoted my kindness was replaced by pure disgust. I barely remembered my own mother's warnings, but her wisdom now took hold.

"I need you to go," I said.

"Go?" she asked, "You just arrived. I need to know everything."

"I need you to go," I said again. "Please just go."

I saw her smiling face turn dark and instead of standing in shame, I saw her face turn sour as she continued to stare examining my face for a clue to my motivations toward her.

"The Lady has asked you to leave," Willa said moving her large body backing Brigit from the room.

"I'll let you rest. We can talk later," Brigit said over Willa's shoulder.

"Not in this lifetime," I said to the room that Brigit just left. I heard the slightest of laugh escaping Willa as she closed the door to my chamber shutting out my past.

"Now let's get you back to your life," she turned clapping her big hands.

CHAPTER 18

I greeted my husband differently than I had imagined. I left my anger and hurt behind as I stood straight and confident. I wasn't the same naïve young girl who traded her country for her heart. My father was a king and my mother a queen, and I now stood on my own land as a simple wife of a knight. No longer would I be an innocent bystander in my own life.

"Nesta," he said rushing to me and putting both hands on my shoulders looking into my eyes. I didn't resist his gaze and returned the tenderness, tears not even threatening to fall. I showed my husband a sweet smile that hid the fire that burned deep inside.

He embraced me and I returned the affection by resting my head for a few seconds on his chest. I breathed in his familiar scent and closed my eyes, forcing the memories of a time before Owain to guide me into my future.

I pulled back to look into his serious eyes. "Gerald, you look well." My words fell easily from my lips. "I am just so grateful to be home."

"I was afraid I would never see your beautiful face again," he said, touching my cheek with the back of his hand. I pushed last night's memory as far back as I could. I knew I couldn't continue my life if I let the resentment take over as he has had to release his own resentment of a King who invaded his castle so many times, claiming his wife as his mistress. I imagined Henry's determination toward my return was just another humiliation that Gerald would have to suffer. I could hardly blame his frustrations and considered that perhaps his dalliance with

Brigit somehow allowed him to move beyond that humiliation.

"I am grateful to King Henry as he is most responsible for your safe return," he said as if he was reading my mind.

I didn't respond to the subject of Henry as I didn't want to review my journey home that included a visit to court in London.

"Oh, my dear husband," I smiled, "there is so much to be done to get things back in order, but I can no longer endure another moment without putting my eyes on my sons." I turned before he could respond. "We can speak more at the evening meal," I said as I walked away. On my way out, I signaled Hait who was waiting at the end of the hall.

As soon as Hait caught up with me and I was sure we were far enough from Gerald's ears, I told him, "Get rid of Brigit."

"What should I do with her?" he asked.

"Throw her naked in the nettles for all I care," I said watching Hait's eyes grow wide, "or you can deliver her to the far path away from the castle and make sure the guards know she is never allowed entrance inside these walls again and give her this." I handed him a small bag of coins I pulled from my front pocket and a bracelet I'd removed from my wrist.

The bracelet was one of my most valued possessions. It had been a token of friendship when Brigit and I had sat under the same willow tree where we had first met, pledging our friendship forever, each cutting a section of our long hair, carefully dividing it and braiding the sections of blonde and red into a tight-laced braid. I once imagined us as old woman watching our grandchildren play together, but this morning when I looked into her face, I saw betrayal, a reminder of all that I had lost since then. I was no longer an innocent little girl giving my heart away so freely.

"As you wish," Hait said smiling as if he was going to enjoy this task.

"After that, I need you to take a message to the King," I said handing him a small scroll tied with a red ribbon and sealed with my Welsh family seal.

Hait bowed his head in acknowledgement before leaving my side. But instead of watching Brigit be dragged out the front gate, I decided to reunite with my sons whom I was sure wouldn't be the little boys I left behind for what seemed like such a long time ago.

I had almost given up hope that my letter to the King had made any impact until Hait rode up with a small contingent of men. My heart pounded in my chest with anticipation. A whole season had passed with no word, so I doubted anything would change until I recognized a young man riding next to Hait. It was my dear brother, Gruffydd. It had been years since I had laid eyes on the teenage boy, now a full-grown man. I felt tears well up but kept my resolve to never let them fall again.

As soon as they reached me, Gruffydd leapt from his horse and picked me from my feet like I was a feather. Gerald had joined me to greet the unexpected King's men and looked a bit puzzled as he accepted the parchment roll from Hait with the King's seal. I watched out of the corner of my eye as Gerald read the message at the same time fussing over my brother.

"You have no idea how happy I am to see you, brother," I said to Gruffydd, holding his huge muscular arm. He had no remnants of boyhood left.

"It seems you will not be rid of me anytime soon, sister. I have been assigned to serve under your husband, Sir Gerald, on behalf of the King," he said smiling, "and I hear rumors it is of your doing." I knew I should have told Gerald of my message to the King, but I chose to hold my tongue in case it never happened.

Gerald looked to me and Hait before holding out his hand to my brother. "Welcome back to Wales," he said as they shook hands. I knew he would need an explanation later but for now I was basking in the joy of the presence of my dear brother.

"It's good to be home." Gruffydd took a deep breath as if it were the first breath, he had taken in all the years he spent in Ireland.

"Tell me, brother, how is our mother?" I watched my

brothers face fall.

"Oh Nesta, you didn't know?"

"Know what?"

"She was lost soon after she crossed into Ireland." Gruffydd hung his head. "She came on a ship just after I arrived but was very ill and didn't even recognize me. She passed peacefully and I am sure looks down on us proudly."

"So much has been kept from my ears, dear brother. We will have to take some time to bridge the time we have been apart," I said this with an edge to my voice to show my displeasure with my husband whom I was sure knew everything but had said nothing. Gerald didn't flinch as I am sure he had issues with the secrets I also kept.

"It seems the Welsh rule has also increased," Gerald said, interrupting our reunion. "It seems the King has reinstated the lands to Owain's father, Cadwygan. He is convinced of his innocence in having any part of your abduction and believes this will provide some relief in the uprisings in the region."

Hait added, "It has already had a calming effect in the North and we have been able to bring most of our soldiers back to ready for trouble again brewing in Normandy."

I couldn't help smiling to myself. I had convinced Henry to restore Cadwygan and allow my brother to safely return to our lands. This was only step one of my plan, and I knew I needed to take action soon as the lands we stood on rightfully belonged to my brother but was currently under my own husband's control.

"You are not safe," I said quietly, even though I knew there was no one that could overhear our conversation.

"I am fully aware of my situation, sister." Gruffydd smiled at me as if he already knew my plans. "The moment I stepped onto the ship; I knew my life was in your hands. Hait convinced me the King would place me safely into your care, but I am not here to serve your Norman Lord, I assure you."

"I didn't think you would," I smiled as I spoke still quietly.

"I have made alliances with Owain and we have made

contact with Daffydd ap Cynan for an additional alliance."

"I am relieved to hear that you have not been idle during your time in exile."

"Far from it, Nesta. I have trained every day for having an opportunity to reclaim what was our father's," he said.

"It is a delicate thing we have here, Gruffydd," I said carefully. "Henry values peace over war and his holding of all England and Normandy has stretched his forces beyond his purse, so compelling peace with additional financial support will appear as a benefit."

"It seems the Norman Lords have creeped into our lands, setting castles about claiming our best lands for themselves," he said.

"It does no good when our people resist, attacking those castles, steeling cattle, burning crops, and refusing to serve their households. It has been chaos, and the one thing Henry can't tolerate is chaos. He needs the Welsh resistance to stop and I have given him a solution. You, my dear brother, is part of the solution," I said proudly.

"I hate to disappoint you, Nesta, I am not here for peace. I am here to take my lands back. I am here to save my people."

"I know you are, that is why I was desperate for your return. But your nephews are also of Norman blood and they will need to find a peace in the end, and I am begging you to help me find the peace for our country that has been torn apart since our ancestors fought each other instead of banding together to fight off the invaders. We have a chance to correct history in our lifetime."

"I agree we need all of our regions to join forces to keep Wales for our children. Owain assures me that his father is committed to the country of Powys, and I will go to Daffydd with our plans."

"Very well but keep any specifics to your most trusted advisors. The King pays his spies well," I said.

"How can I explain a trip to the country of Gwynedd?"

"I will take care of that," I said confidently.

My conversation with Gerald wasn't as easy as I had hoped. He started by slamming the door behind him as he entered my chamber. He was usually mild mannered, so it was obvious I was about to feel the full force of his anger like I had never seen before.

"How dare you go behind my back with Henry. Don't you think I have suffered enough humiliation at your hand?" His face was red, and his rage was so intense I thought he might raise his hand to me. I didn't say a thing but backed up to my bed, trying to put some distance between us, but if I took a step back, he took a step forward, staying close to my face.

"I may not be a King or a Welsh Prince, but I am your Lord, Nesta! You are my wife, and you will not go behind my back, negotiate on my behalf, or communicate ever again with the King in any form without my permission." He backed up a few steps as he let the final few words fall from his lips. "I have had enough!" He turned to leave.

"You have had enough?" I said loudly causing him to freeze and turn to face me. I had never spoke back to him, but I was resolved to stand my ground. "My soul was dead when I met you. I had no purpose. I had resolved to my prescribed life but now I accept my life has never belonged to me but was always dictated by the blood of my ancestors that soak the earth beneath my feet." I took a step closer and stood tall to Gerald, who hadn't moved whether in shock or resolve. I continued, "My loyalty must be to this Welsh land that exists from generations of sacrifice. The sacrifice I now give willingly is not without heartbreak as I must leave my very soul in your hands as I leave this place of comfort for a likely tragic end. Please remember me as I was and not what I must become."

Without another word and without any energy left, Gerald turned to leave but when he reached the door, he stopped and turned to look at me. I stood in the same position, frozen and afraid to move. His face had changed to a curious smile. I was confused but he just shook his head and left, carefully closing the door as if he was sneaking out in the middle of the night.

CHAPTER 19

It wasn't long before Gerald's anger cooled to me and we were able to speak about household issues at the same time he seemed to be getting along with Gruffydd quite well. Gruffydd wisely brought him close and exposed a few secret forest pathways and the best hunting spots in Deheubarth as any good brother-in-law would.

Gruffydd even traveled with Gerald to a nearby stronghold and easily negotiated a peaceful resolution with the local Welshmen uprising.

The surrounding landowners were happy with their Norman Lord because of his peaceful nature, and he was known for fair resolutions as well as his marriage to their Welsh Princess and now the presence of Gruffydd, whom they saw as their rightful king.

"I am going to Gwynedd," Gruffydd told me as we met in the garden after the evening meal.

"How did you convince Gerald to grant you the freedom to go?" I asked Gruffydd.

"The uprising by the villages at the river Tywi where the boatmen and the villagers were blocking the Norman ship from docking. I spoke with the leader of the uprising and convinced them to back away," he said.

"Why would they be blocking a ship?" I asked.

"I'm not sure but there have been a lot of disruptions lately. I heard there may be a contingent sent from Gwynedd to block trade to Deheubarth," he said smiling.

"Really?"

"Gerald suggested I travel north to investigate and stop such a campaign."

"I agreed to make this trip and promised positive results."

"You are a genius, Gruffydd," I said.

"But what about the disruptions at the coast?"

"Those disrupters will be by my side as I travel north."

"It was your allies making the trouble?"

"How else could I prove my worth to Gerald?" he said standing.

I watched as my brother and four others left through the front gates, not sure when I would ever see him again. Over the last few months, he had again become my closest friend, as if we were back in our childhood where we relied on each other for support.

Time went by and no word from my brother caused Gerald to complain and threaten to send word to the King.

"There is no sign of treason," I said.

"Then he should have turned up dead," Gerald said.

"Why do you say such things?" I turned away from Gerald but not before he reached out and grabbed my arm roughly, causing me to yep.

"You better not have anything to do with this. I watched you two conspire in the garden. The devil only knows what you two cooked up," he said letting go of my arm just as the castle bells rang indicating an arrival.

I looked out the open window. "It's Hait," I said.

"Of course, it is," he said, "another one of your admirers."

I ignored my husband's remarks and walked to the courtyard to greet Hait. Gerald was only half right. I knew Hait had a soft heart toward me, but I had never acknowledged the feelings even as I always felt protected whenever he was near, especially as I felt unprotected by my husband since the return of my brother.

The greeting with Hait was not what I expected. He turned his head from me coldly and avoiding me and spoke directly to Gerald.

"I have urgent business with you, my Lord," he said. He was hiding something, and I suddenly had a rush of worry. I followed him to Gerald's study where I was shut out. There was something wrong and it involved me, I was sure.

I waited outside the door, trying to hear anything but could only make out muffled words, nothing clear enough to satisfy my curiosity until the meeting broke and the men filed out. I heard my brother's name. Gerald and Hait stayed behind, apparently looking at a map. I walked in and neither bothered to look up.

"If Gruffydd has moved his men into the mountains, it will be almost impossible to locate them," Hait said pointing to a section of the map.

"I don't understand how he assembled that many troops," Gerald said.

"It was his wife that had already had a following," Hait said. "She is called Gwenllian, the fourth daughter of Daffydd and the leader of the most effective rebellion."

"His wife!" I said aloud. Both men looked at me at the same time. Hait was flushed but Gerald wore a calm look on his face. Hait looked at Gerald for permission to speak and Gerald responded with a slight shrug.

"It seems your brother has been busy," Hait said, "as soon as he arrived at Gwynedd, he was made aware of a plot against him. Apparently, Daffydd had been paid to betray him by King Henry."

"How did Henry even know Gruffydd was there?" I looked at Gerald who had returned his attention to the map. The silence of both men was my answer. My husband was not the fool we had assumed and had reported my brother's travels to Henry, whom I was sure took it as a threat and an excuse to arrest him or even kill him.

"Daffydd's daughter, Gwenllian, found out that her father plotted against Gruffydd and not only warned him but also took him into the mountains where she had already organized the largest Welsh rebellion force, we have ever known. The two have conspired and now command the forces together as man and wife," Hait further explained.

"So, you are saying, the greatest Welsh rebellion in our history is led by a woman?" I was really stating it to myself, "The wife of my brother?" Again, both men stayed silent. I turned in time to hide my wide smile. I could hardly contain my joy. I knew at that moment that my brother would be reinstated as the rightful King of Deheubarth.

I could barely contain myself the rest of the day. I tried to imagine the woman who controlled a Welsh rebellion. It was obvious my husband and Hait were now enemies of my brother and would kill him if they had the chance. I was just lucky that my sons were still too young to ride with their father against my brother.

It was a quiet morning with just a few of the men left for protection, which I didn't really need. I packed a basket full of fresh bread, fruit, and dried meats. I had my heavy cloak wrapped around me as I mounted my palfrey.

"I don't think it's a good idea to ride in the wood alone, my Lady." Willa stood next to the horse, handing the basket up to me.

"Honestly, Willa, I need a good ride through the forest to clear my head, but you need not worry for my safety. I have been riding these woods since I was a young girl. The trails are as familiar to me as the halls of this castle," I said and pulled up my skirt, exposing a small dagger strapped to my calf. "And if some wild one attempts to take me by surprise in my own wood, they will find a path to the south gate sooner than later."

"I will be watching the sun and if it sets before your return, I will send the guards to search for you," she said. I suddenly felt a panic rise in my chest.

"Promise me, Willa, you won't tell anyone I have gone or where I am going."

"But I am sure you will be noticed leaving the gate," she said confused.

"I will be leaving out the side gate and wish to remain

invisible."

"Why the secret exit, my Lady?"

"There is no secret, just a wish to be left alone, and I believe Gerald left instructions to keep a close eye on me while he is away. I do not wish to be followed about."

"Okay, Nesta, just be careful and promise to return before the sun falls."

"I promise," I said as I pulled the reigns, leading my horse south, away from the front gate. I didn't look back but kept a slow trot so as to not create a dust trail or any attention my way.

The woods were active with bird song and small animals scurrying in the bushes as I passed. I listen carefully for the sound of another horse or footsteps that may have followed me, but this forest of my youth welcomed my appearance and folded her arms around me, protecting me from the world that had stolen me from her.

The deeper I went, the more my shoulders dropped, and I could breathe into my lungs a life lived long ago. The paths were narrow and almost disappeared at several points until finally there was no path but a clearing with a small stream to rest and let my horse drink while I found a large rock near a giant oak.

The rock had a mark that looked like an arrow on a thick crooked shaft. It was Gruffydd and I who made this symbol our secret message. It represented the tail of our Welsh Lion. I struggled to move the rock but had to use a large stick to leverage it enough to reach under. I found the flattened rolled parchment and unrolled it but was disappointed that it was written with my own hand. Gruffydd had not received the message. I took a new roll hidden below the food in my basket and delivered it into the hiding spot, once again using the stick as leverage.

I was disappointed but I still had two more chances to receive a reply. I continued my journey until I reached the small waterfall where Gruffydd and I would play on the hot summer days, jumping into the freezing cold basin of the falls. I looked around for anyone before I walked behind the falls to a small cave.

It was wet and cold, but I found the symbol on a flat rock. When I lifted the rock, the parchment was again the one I had left. I again replaced it with a new message. The excitement I felt when I left this morning was replaced by disappointment. Gruffydd hadn't received my messages. I had one more chance, but my heart was now in a shadow of depression. I had hoped to help my brother but failed.

I ate a few bites of the bread and drank some wine before I got back on my horse to check the third spot, the least likely because it was so close to Pembroke. If Gruffydd was in the woods, he wouldn't be traveling alone, and I am sure the number of men would cause attention, but I still had a slight hope that my brother would have seen my message.

The last spot was beneath the very willow tree where I had met Brigit for the first time. I had taken Gruffydd there to show him where I had spent that night. I had told him it was like a giant fairy garden where all the branches reached the ground. I told him about the magic I felt when I was there. Our secret symbol was carved in the trunk of the tree just before it entered the earth. I cleared away all the small leaves and dry willow branches I used to cover the small hole I had dug. This parchment was in perfect shape, since it hadn't been smashed by a stone. But as I brought it forth, I once again recognized it was the same as the other two. I sat defeated with my back to the trunk, fighting tears of disappointment when I heard the rustle of a horse on the dried leaves outside my hiding spot. It might have been my horse got loose from where I had tethered her on a nearby path, but I stayed still in case it was a stranger. I shallowed my breath so I could hear my own heartbeat until it jumped out of my chest into a small scream as the curtain of branches parted and a small man broke through. But it wasn't a man at all, it was a woman dressed as a man. But when she removed her hood, I saw she was beautiful, and her white skin was almost glowing. I had to blink several times to make sure I wasn't dreaming but when she held out her hand. I took it easily as she lifted me to a standing position.

"Sister," she said, "I am Gwenllian, wife of Gruffydd."

"I am Nesta," I said weakly as I was taken aback by the lightness of her clear blue eyes. It was like looking into a clear morning sky. Her hair was auburn, and she had it in a long braid that reached well passed her belt.

"You are so beautiful," I said.

Gwenllian smiled broadly. "As are you, Nesta," she said.

"How did you know I was here?"

"I followed you from the falls," she said in a low tone.

"But…"

"We received your message but did not respond in case it was a trick," she said.

"Where is Gruffydd?"

"He could not travel this far. The King has a large bounty on his head and has bribed even the most dedicated Welshman, including my own father. He threatens to confiscate their lands or imprison them if found that they have provided any aid to the rebellion."

"But the rebellion is growing," I said. "I have overheard my husband talking with the other lords. They are all worried."

"As they should be," she said as she stood straighter. "We have already taken down several Norman holdings." I noticed her hand touch the scabbard of the sword that hung on her side. They were not hands of a maiden but obviously toughened by battle. I was suddenly jealous of this woman who was the leader of a rebellion while I sat in my comforts, waiting for results.

"I am here to be of assistance," I told her. "I have direct access to the King, and of course my husband is a key figure in his service."

"Those facts are well known, my Lady," she said, "and for that reason I am here."

"Of course," I said. I knelt down to my basket and handed her a thick slice of bread and some dried meat. She took it with confusion but bit into the bread. I continued to dig deep into the basket when I pulled several parchments from the false bottom and handed them to her.

"What's this?" she asked.

"I copied all the maps and correspondence I could. They are not perfect, but it is what I could get."

"This is treason," she said.

"It is not treason to my King," I said, "Gruffydd is the true King of Deheubarth and I am the daughter of the slayed King taken prisoner by the Norman invaders."

"You steal these from under your husband's nose? Don't you think him to be suspicious?"

"He doesn't think I am capable, more like I am weak, but I have been a dutiful wife and I am the mother of his children. I don't think he suspects anything."

"Nesta, you have to be sure these documents are reliable. There is no way he forged some plan to tempt you to feed your brother these plans?"

"I admit, Gerald is a strategic thinker, but I have to say he has a weakness, and that is he underestimates me and my loyalty to my lands."

"Do you not love your husband?"

"I love him as much as I can, but I betrayed my people a long time ago, and now I need to correct history, so if it means my husband as a sacrifice, so be it. The only thing I care for more are my sons."

"But the Norman blood also runs through their veins," Gwenllian said, her blue eyes wide.

"And I hope that their blood will never be spilled in these times. I hope that it is their lives that can preserve the language of my ancestors. I need their support to be with my brother, your husband, the rightful King."

"So, we will meet when we can. Leave the messages under the falls. We will check as often as possible." Gwenllian reached over me and embraced me in a tight hug. The strong leather smell of her vest and the light metal cold against my body reminded me of our worlds so far apart, but I now had a part in my history.

CHAPTER 20

Early summer was my favorite season to travel the roads where the forest met the sea, where the English roads would welcome our carriage with a flat surface, providing a smoother path instead of during spring travel, where the heavy wheels carved out wide ruts that filled with rain where an unskilled driver would lose at least one wheel on the long journey.

I never complained about the rain because I knew the earth's thirst after a long summer once quenched, provided the soil to loosen enough for the seeds to reach out toward the sun and flourish in fields of grain which now surrounded us, moving in waves with the soft breeze.

I always enjoyed travel away from my daily existence, especially these days on the empty road where my soul was free, and each breath filled me with the scent of wildflowers and pine. We reached the brininess of the sea, where the air was filled with a foggy mist and it was like riding through a cloud. The mornings were brisk, and I rode with a winter cloak until the sun was full in the sky and warmed my bones enough to free me of the heavy cloak.

As we came closer to England, the freedom of the forest disappeared, and the weight of my responsibilities hung heavy on my shoulders. The last few days of the journey took us along well traveled roads littered with small villages where I would find some reason to stop, whether to break our fast or enjoy an evening wine. I took my time at each of these small communities against the wishes of my guards, but they were easily manipulated with tankards of ale and fresh meat pies while I busied myself searching for gossip from the locals. Most of the information was merely complaints of their Lords and not useful, but I found a few tidbits to tuck away.

Our arrival at Westminster was delayed by just a few days but our welcome did not suffer. As we rode through the gate, we were received by soldiers in full regalia, a number of household staff, some of which I recognized from my youth, but it was the young man who stood in front of the entourage who took my breath away.

Had it been so long since I laid eyes on my son, I couldn't recognize this youth. As patiently as possible, I exited the carriage, my son's hand there to assist me. As I stood, I could no longer resist and wrapped my arms around his broad shoulders.

"Oh Henry, my beautiful boy," I said pulling back from him enough to look at his face that was above my own.

"Mother," he said, "you look as radiant as the sun and more mysterious than the moon."

"My son has inherited his father's charms, I see." I smiled but as I said it, I felt a small twinge of regret for what I was doing to his father as well as my son. I needed to figure out how to keep my son away from the damage and at the same time be loyal to my obligations. He might resemble his Norman father, but he also had the blood of a Welsh king running through his veins.

"Come, Mother, you must get settled and ready. My father would like to see you before this evening."

"Your father is here?"

"Yes, I thought you knew. They are celebrating the marriage of my sister, Matilda, and the future Holy Roman Emperor," he said in a sarcastic tone. "The hall will be quite full of conspiracists this evening."

"I see," I said slowly, but my mind raced with possibilities. There would be much information floating through the crowded hall. I was sure I could gather enough information to aid the rebellion, but I knew I had to be cautious. Being too interested in the movements of the court would cause suspicion.

Before Henry left my side, he stood erect in front of me smiling and grabbed both my shoulders with his large hands and kissed each of my cheeks. In that moment, I saw a reflection of his father, remembering a lifetime ago when I was in love with the fourth son of the King and my future had promise of a much different outcome but here, I stood plotting against my first love.

There were several unfamiliar faces that greeted us as the ladies showed me to my room, Martha was the maid assigned to me and took care to introduce each dignitary as we were greeted, and when out of earshot, explained their background story so I would have perspective. Instantly, I knew Martha was a key to my motivations.

A beautiful young girl dressed in a light blue dress with an elegantly embroidered neckline and sleeves stopped in the hall with a slight curtsy and then stood solid in front of us.

"My Lady Nesta, may I present the Lady Adeliza, daughter of Godfrey, Duke of Louvain," Martha said.

"You're quite beautiful, my dear," I said to the young girl wondering if young Henry had his eye on this one. She was stunning with blond hair and the beautiful brown eyes of a confident doe.

"As are you, my Lady," her voice low but confident.

"I hope we can speak later," I said as she stepped aside to let us through.

"I as well," she said with a small curtsy as we passed.

As soon as we were well down the hall, Martha spoke up in a conspiratorial whisper. "I think Henry has his eyes on that one."

"Really?" I raised an eyebrow. "I think they are close to the same age."

Martha laughed. "Not your son, Henry. The King, Henry."

"Not a surprise," I said rolling my eyes enlisting a conspirator's giggle from the girl.

I looked back to Lady Adeliza and remembered a time when Henry and I started our affair. My blood boiled not with jealousy but the manipulation and broken promises of a man whose only goal was to conquer the world. But ultimately, it was I who allowed him to lift my skirt as I was a willing participant mesmerized by his words. I lost my innocence and weakened my country. Even if I could befriend this girl and have a say, I knew the power of Henry's words were too strong to resist. Instead, I will pity her.

My room was the same one I stayed in when I was a "guest" under King William's foster and anytime I had visited over the years, so there was some comfort of familiarity. The room was welcoming with a small fire in the hearth that could be stoked later to combat the evening chill. The burning embers brought back the memory of that poor boy who used to deliver the coals and was brutalized by William for the poor boy's father's land.

I shook these memories from my head and sorted through my gowns until I found a soft pink with white rabbit fur sewn into the pleats. I carefully tied my plaits up on top of my head, making sure the soft lines of my neck were exposed. I knew Henry's weaknesses and I was determined to take full advantage of them while I had his attention.

Martha and I chatted as she helped me prepare myself. She continued to name the expected guests and filled in any bits of rumor that accompanied them. She knew more about each of these people than their own kin. She finally cinched the last ties around my waist, leaving a beautiful bow accent that would surely draw attention to my backside.

"How do you know so much?" I asked.

"I am so low-born, my Lady, that I am invisible to most people here in court," she said. "As long as their cups are full and I stay silent, their lips are moving."

"Why are you telling me all of this? Are you not afraid I could report you?"

Martha laughed, "I know who you are!"

"Who I am?" I asked nervously.

"You are Nesta, Princess of Deheubarth, sister of Gruffydd," she said confidently. I breathed a sigh of relief before she added in a whisper, "My brother, Myryn, is part of the resistance."

"Are you Welsh?" I asked.

"Of course, I'm Welsh, Lady Nesta. Most of the servants are Welsh or Flemish. There aren't too many true Britons left."

"But your name is Martha?"

"Not my true name," she said again with the smile, "have to stay invisible."

I nodded my head in understanding and was glad for an ally but kept my mouth shut as I knew all too well how Henry paid spies. Many a Welshman had turned on one another for even the smallest bag of Henry's coin.

Martha led me to the King's outer chamber and relinquished me to the guard with a silent curtsey. She took a few steps back and leaned against a wall. I imagined she would stay to escort me back after my meeting with Henry.

As I entered the chamber, I saw Henry bent over his desk with a quill upright as he made some marks on a parchment. I stood silent next to his guard waiting for his acknowledgement. When he finally looked up, he jumped from his seat and came around to face me.

"My dear Nesta," he said kissing me straight on the lips. I couldn't bring myself to respond but stood in anticipation.

"My King," I said as I curtseyed low to him. When I rose and looked at him, he was motioning the guard to leave us.

He stood with his feet apart and his hands on his hips staring at me. I watched him examine my curves and his eyes settle on my bare neck before he looked back into my eyes. I took the time to also examine him. I must have forgotten his age because seeing my son reminded me of Henry's in his youth. Now, I saw a weathered face with lines around the eyes and hair even thinner than before that had turned completely grey. He was even plumper than the last time I saw him, and his belly fell way past his belt.

"Nesta, you look like a goddess," Henry said.

"Thank you, Henry," I said sweetly.

"It's been so long," he said as his eyes again traveled down my body. He reached out to touch the rabbit fur and kept his hand on my hip. I stood close and batted my eyes slowly, giving him permission. "You are so beautiful, my love," he said softly in my ear before he kissed my neck. I tried to regulate my breath but when his lips touched my ear, I felt a shiver of recognition to a long-lost emotional connection to this man but did not let it interfere with my absolution in the task I must perform.

He broke away for a moment and took my hand, led me into his inner chamber where he laid me onto his bed, not even bothering to move the furs. He kissed me and I kissed him back trying hard to show passion when my heart was truly cold to him.

He didn't take long to untie the carefully laced gown and throw it to the floor, at the same time removing his own robes. I became a willing participant and easily yielded to him as he lifted my shift and attempted to enter me. His manliness was too soft so I reached down to massage it enough so he could penetrate me. I moved with him as he entered me, and I faked pleasure as he grunted on top of me. I knew Henry's every move and I played along like I had many times in the past. This was my payment to the King but this time, I would ask for favors.

When Henry finally rolled off me panting in exhaustion, I laid next to him, letting his hand rest on my naked breast. When his breath was steady, I leaned on my elbow to face him. He still had sweat on his brow and his full face looked up at me with a satisfied smile.

"Henry, you are still the man I remember," I said.

"You will always have my heart in your hands, my lovely Nesta," he said.

"I need a favor," I said.

"Really?" Henry sat up and his smile widened. "A favor?"

"Henry, really," I sat to face him, "I am serious."

"Okay," he said, "how can I please my beautiful Princess Nesta? That is, unless it is to provide you additional pleasure, I might need a bit of a rest." He said, laughing too loud while I fought to control my eye roll.

"Henry, please…" I said, "it's Gruffydd—"

"Stop!" Henry's face turned red and he climbed out of the bed. "Do you know where he is, Nesta?" Henry was now the King again.

"No," I said, "How would I know where he is?"

Henry's face changed but he still looked confused. "What do you want, then?"

"Henry, I ask for myself and my children that you restore Deheubarth to my brother as its King. It is his rightful—"

"Stop!" Henry was red with fury. "Your brother has caused the worst rebellion in history. He is attacking our holdings, causing damage to our property and I guarantee he will be defeated. I will have his head and the head of his wife."

"Henry…"

"I said stop!" Henry raised his hand as if he was about to strike me when all of a sudden, he froze, and the fury left his face. I wasn't sure whether he understood or he changed his tactics. "Why are you asking for such a favor?"

"It's not for me or even my brother," I said softly, "It's for my husband, Gerald, and my sons. We just want peace. The rebels threaten our borders and the lives of my children. I just remember the peace when your father and my father had a mutual relationship and we paid fealty and maintained peace with the Welsh. There would be no reason for rebellion."

Henry kept his eyes on me. I watched his face change as he was trying to decide my motivations.

"Henry, my children are Norman blood, they are the sons of your most loyal Knight. Has Gerald not served you well?"

Henry took a long breath and sat next to me. "Nesta, I understand you think you have an idea of what could bring peace, but I assure you, you have no idea how men think, and if I announced a new King in Wales, it would cause another rebellion. Believe me, your sons are safe, and I will get a hold of this rebellion before the New Year begins. I have a plan."

I bit the inside of my lip, causing the metallic taste of

blood to fill my mouth. How dare he think I am so stupid, but now I had an advantage! I was playing a stupid woman, but I imagined I was a warrior like my sister-in-law, only without the armor. I bowed my head toward Henry.

"Thank you, Henry." I said. He patted me on the head like I was his child as he pulled on his trousers. I kept my head bent so my fury couldn't be seen. As soon as he left, I leapt up and dressed. Martha came in and silently helped me put myself back together.

My son, Henry, escorted me into the hall that evening and showed me to my seat at a table set for the landholders and since Gerald wasn't with me, I was seated near other single ladies. The room was full of people from all over England, Scotland, Wales, and other foreign lands evident by the unfamiliar languages spoken all around me. This was definitely an event to bring people from the far ends of the earth.

CHAPTER 21

Henry and Edith were seated on the dais, and they were silently observing the room. Edith was already a small woman but appeared even smaller sitting next to an expanded Henry. Next to Edith sat now Empress Matilda and her new husband, the Holy Roman Emperor, Henry V. The last time I saw Matilda was when she was six years old, right before she was betrothed and shipped to Germany. It was a hard time for England and Wales as it created additional taxes in order to pay her exorbitant dowry.

On Henry's right sat Prince William Adelin, the legitimate son and heir to the English throne. Prince William resembled his mother, small in stature and looking small seated next to Henry. Sitting next to William was a tall, handsome young man who looked familiar, but I couldn't quite place his familiarity until I looked to his right and saw my son Henry. As the realization hit me, I almost fell out of my chair.

It was Robert, my first-born son, the baby boy taken from my arms so long ago. My mind raced as the questions flooded my mind: Did he even know who I was? Has Henry told him of his mother? It took everything I had to keep seated. I couldn't stop staring at my son now a man, but I also had to concentrate on my task. My head was swimming and suddenly unfocused. I took a long drink of the strong ale that sat in front of me cursing Henry who had not prepared me for this shock.

"Where is Gerald?" asked Alice de Clermont, breaking my thoughts of my boy. I took a deep breath as my head continued to spin. I needed to focus.

"He stayed in our region for the King's business," I said. "And your husband?"

"He is at gathering troops at Cardigan," she said.

"Troops for Normandy?" I asked.

"Normandy?" she furrowed her brows, "Why would you think that?"

"I thought there was an unrest," I said innocently. "I heard Gerald speaking with his men and—"

"It's the savages," she interrupted me.

"The savages?" I acted confused but knew exactly what she was saying.

"The Welsh," she said. "We are finally going to rid ourselves of those natives."

"I heard they are a threat to all of us," I said innocently.

"If they survive the next year, I will be surprised," she said.

"I am afraid each day that the rebels will take our land," I said, and she looked at me with a serious eye. She looked around the room before speaking and putting her hand close to my ear. She told me that her husband, Gilbert fitz Richard, would lead a force from the South near Deheubarth. Alexander, King of Scotland, would come from the North, and King Henry would press from mid Wales. The plan was to force the rebels into the open and kill their leaders.

Didn't this woman realize my brother and his wife were the leaders? Was this a trick? Did Henry seat me next to this woman with a motive? I looked up and saw Henry looking at us and his face was worried. Did he know this woman knew his secret plans? Did he know I was a spy? When we were alone earlier, why didn't he tell me my son was in attendance? I was tired of Henry's ambitions.

The meal finally ended, freeing me from my seat but not without valuable information, which was my original reason for attending even though the source was unexpected. I still wasn't convinced the information wasn't shared purposely, but I would work to validate it before passing it to the rebels.

Before I could leave the hall, I was cornered by Henry, who still had a worried look on his face.

"I see you suffered the company of Lady Clermont," he said.

"If I have to hear one more detail of her Spring Ball, I will die from boredom. Did you know she is requesting each couple to match in color? I can't imagine Gerald ever wearing light blue, maybe a soft pink," I said.

"Ridiculous," he said smiling in relief.

"Henry, I do have an issue and am furious with you," I said.

"My Lady?"

"My son," I said looking over his shoulder. "Why did you not prepare me for such a shock?"

"I wanted to surprise you," he said.

"I hate you at this moment," I said. "Please don't torture me further."

Henry just smiled and motioned to Robert. Both Robert and another young man similar in age approached us.

"Princess Nesta of Deheubarth, may I present my son Robert, Earl of Gloucester, and Sir Richard of Lincoln, both my sons raised by Robert Bloet, Bishop of Lincoln."

"Robert," I said ignoring Henry and Richard, "do you not know who I am?"

Robert reached for my hand, kissed the top of it, and bowed slightly, "I believe you to be my mother," he said softly.

I could not contain my tears and they fell freely. He gently wiped the tears with the back of his hand. "Please don't cry," he said helplessly.

"I am sorry, I have just wished for this day since the day you were taken from me. I have had a hole in my heart that has been filled in this moment," I said, noticing the other two men had disappeared, leaving us to share this moment of reunion.

"You did not know where I was?"

"No, it was for your protection," I said.

"My father had always kept me well informed of you and even provided a portrait that I kept by my bedside throughout my life. I have it still."

I reached up to touch his face, so grateful my son had grown into such a handsome man.

"We have so much to talk about," I said. "I can't wait to find out every little thing about your life. I feel like I have missed so much."

"Brother," my son Henry called, motioning to Robert.

"We can talk long into the night if you wish, Mother, but I will excuse myself to my brother's needs for the moment, if you will allow."

"Of course, my dear son, we will talk soon," I said. He hugged my shoulders and moved across the room as I watched him leave with new hope for the future.

I spent the next few days getting to know my son, but I knew I needed to pass on the information Lady Clermont had unwittingly provided me.

"I hate to leave you," I said, "but I need to get back to your brothers before they burn the stables to the ground."

"I look forward to meeting my brothers soon," Robert said as he opened the door to the carriage.

"I promise to return soon with the boys," I said, kissing him on the cheek before I entered the carriage. I took one last look at his face, trying to burn it into my memory as the door closed and the horses jerked us forward.

We made several stops to villages along the way, and I left pieces of the information with trusted allies but never the full plan as a precaution.

I was never sure if the information reached Gwenllian or my brother, but the rebellion grew over the next few years, forcing Henry to even pull his forces from Normandy to combat the rebels in Wales. Even with the increased forces, the great Welsh rebellion held.

The hope for a restored Wales was heavy on my mind. I would continue to fight for independence. I would keep myself entrenched in the politics of the land as much as I could.

The opportunity came on 25 November 1120 when I took my sons to London where we could experience the arrival of the White Ship, known to be the fastest ship in England. The ship was expected to arrive that evening, but the weather seemed to delay her. Robert had accompanied his father, King Henry, on this trip to Normandy and would return on this very ship. Besides checking the progress of a new castle, they would interview possible brides for the young Prince William.

The November afternoon was bitter cold and biting through my cloak, but I was determined to greet Robert as he disembarked the ship. I pulled my hood closed across my face, leaving only enough space for my eyes which kept vigil on the sea.

The crowd was not as patient, and it thinned as the hours passed. And no ship pulled into port. I was about to join the others and retire when the white sails reflected the last of the light from the day. The clouds were thick overhead and seemed to muffle the sounds of the crowd that were reassembling. It wasn't long before disappointment set in that it was clear the ship before us was not the White Ship but another of Henry's vessels flying the King's colors, indicating Henry on board.

The ship docked and the gangway lowered to release the first of the passengers, who was King Henry, closely followed by Robert and Henry, both looking beaten about.

"A rough sea, my Lord?" I heard a dock hand ask the King.

"If one wave missed us, it was by accident. It was as if Poseidon himself had a vendetta and was against us the whole way. It was only when we turned into the channel that we enjoyed some relief," Henry said.

I stayed in the crowd until Henry passed and then moved into view to greet my son, Robert. Robert was a loyal supporter of his father, Henry, and his half-brother, William, the future King of England. There was hardly a time where you wouldn't find Robert near his brother, especially when they traveled across the English Channel to Normandy.

"Hello, Mother," Robert greeted me, his smile perfect.

"I'm so glad for your safe return," I said, "but I was expecting your arrival on Thomas's White Ship."

"My father wanted to detour and visit Gloucester. We left two days prior. The White Ship should have made its way home hours ago," he said looking around as if he didn't immediately notice the ship wasn't docked anywhere nearby.

"That is the word we received too," I said and then remembered the boys who stood near me. "Robert, these are your half-brothers, William, Maurice, and David."

Robert made an exaggerated bow toward the three boys, "Brothers," he acknowledged, "Robert, Earl of Gloucester, at your service."

I was visibly shaking from the cold and Robert must have noticed because he took my arm in his and led us toward the castle. "Let's get in front of the fire so I may get to know my brothers," Robert said smiling.

"That's a great idea," Maurice said as the three boys followed us the short distance to the castle where we were greeted with some hot spiced cider near the hearth. I was relieved of my cloak as were the boys, but my face was chapped from the cold, and I could feel the flush as I sat near the source of heat.

"So, brothers, tell me who is the best archer," Robert said to the three boys who surrounded him like starving baby gulls.

"I am," Maurice said confidently.

"But I am better with a sword, my Lord," said William.

"What about you, young brother?" Robert asked David who flushed at the question.

"His head is stuck in a book when he should be on the field," Maurice said.

"Books?" Robert asked looking at David who nodded silently. "There's nothing wrong with a learned man, dear bother. I was raised by a bishop who had me spend as much time with a book at my nose as with a sword in my hand."

David looked up at his brother and smiled but remained silent.

"Well, my young Lords, Mother," Robert said as he stood, "I must find the reason for the delay of Prince William. We will send a ship at daybreak and I must be rested for the journey."

But just then, the doors were flung open, and several riders accompanied by a middle-aged man, a bit overweight but familiar in his looks, rushed in.

The captain of the guard was the one who stood in front of Henry who had taken his place on a large chair in the center of the room.

"The White Ship has sunk," he said solemnly.

Henry's face went white and he dropped the mug of ale he held.

"Tell me what happened and leave nothing out," Henry said, now standing looking around the soldiers and only spotting the civilian, he stood. "Where is my son?"

"There was but one survivor, my King," the Captain said. "He is the butcher, Berold. We found him clinging onto the rock." The captain pushed the man to confront the King.

"Where is my son?" Henry asked softly.

"I didn't see him myself, my Lord, but I believe he drowned in an attempt to save his sister," Berold, the only known survivor said with his head bent, "I saw him in the life-boat floating but lost sight when he turned back toward the sinking ship."

"Tell me exactly what you did see," the King said, "and leave nothing out."

"The moon was new and the fog so thick that the lanterns barely lit the front of our faces. I was standing alone on the bow when we hit something solid, jerking the ship to a full stop. I stayed where I was, as it was a high point, as the rear started to sink. At first, I thought we were safe but when the crew began to jump ship, I took advantage of my position and jumped to the rocks that we hit, barely in time before the front of the ship also slipped into the sea. I called to others, but the commotion covered my calls. That is when I saw the Prince and Lord Richard get in one of the small lifeboats and clear the wreckage. I could hear more than I could see as most of the lanterns were extinguished as the boat sank. It was the call from his half-sister, Tilly, that must have brought them back. I tried to coax her to the rocks, but she was too panicked to hear my calls. But the Prince must have heard her desperate calls because his lanterned raft turned around, but as he came close, I saw many arms reach from the icy water, clinging to its sides pulling it under, releasing all those who had found safety in its hull. I imagine the second life raft met the same fate. I couldn't see more. I'm so sorry."

Robert was already standing next to Henry and supported him as Henry almost collapsed with both hands over his face. Tears ran down Henry's anguished face, which changed from ruddy red to a pale gray.

The room was silent as we all watched Henry's sad departure, clinging to Robert for support. It was not the first time I witnessed tears fall from Henry's eyes. He was one of the strongest men I knew but his tender heart had been exposed, especially when his children were the subject, legitimate or not.

Henry lost three children that day, Prince William, his heir and two illegitimate children, Richard and Tilly. It was no surprise that young William went back for Tilly. He was known for his attachment to his half-sister.

The death of William Adelin was devastating to Henry as a father as well as for the stability of England, for the laws of succession were no longer in Henry's favor.

CHAPTER 22

It was barely dawn when I heard the approaching horns and sound of horses crossing the castle bridge of my home of Carew. The freshness of the morning was threatening to turn stale as my eyes focused on the familiar banners of the King. The sight of the three golden lions once caused my stomach to flip with excitement, but now it brought bile to my throat. No prior announcement might mean I had been exposed as a traitor but by the time the men came close enough, I once again felt the excitement. Henry had my son, Robert, by his side. They had fewer than a dozen men, all in light armor, so it was definitely a peaceful mission.

I hurried to don a proper dress and shawl and barely made it to the foyer as the King and Robert entered the large wooden doors.

"I'm afraid we didn't receive message of your arrival and have not prepared for such a royal visit, my Lord," Gerald said as he took position by my side. I simply bowed my head to the King and smiled wide at Robert, who returned the gesture.

"We are not here for entertainment or pomp. We have business with your house and did not want to alert the Welsh rebels of our travels, especially with such a small contingent," Henry said stepping in front of me. "It seems our spies are less informed than theirs."

I felt my face turn hot but smiled wide. "I seriously doubt that anyone pays higher than you, my Lord."

"Nesta, hold your tongue before the King," Gerald said.

Henry stared into my eyes, obviously trying to read into

my soul for clues, but I held my secrets tight and was confident they were not revealed.

"It's good to see you, Mother," Robert said, breaking the tension, which seemed to be rooted with the unspoken words between Henry and me. "You look well."

I turned to my son, turning my lips up into a tender smile. "As do you, my son," I said, silently thanking him for the rescue.

"We need to speak privately, Sir Gerald," Henry spoke as he handed his cloak to the waiting servant boy who had appeared. Henry waved him away and the boy moved to collect Robert's cloak before disappearing around the corner.

"Have you broken fast so early this morn?" I asked.

"Some warm ale and Willa's sweet rolls would be a pleasure," Henry said. Unfortunately, Gerald stiffened as he recognized the familiarity of Henry with the household staff as he had spent so much time here when Gerald was away. I motioned toward the entrance to the main hall where several of the household stood waiting for directions. A simple nod sent them to ready the kitchen to prepare for the guests.

Gerald led the two men to the cushioned benches near the hearth where they all settled in front of the fire in full blaze just recently stoked. We were barely settled when the servants delivered plates of boiled figs, apples stuffed with walnuts and honey, and Willa's freshly baked rolls.

I filled three wooden cups with peppered cider and watched the men relax as the cups were emptied and filled several times.

"So, what brings the King all the way to Wales?" Gerald asked innocently. "You could have sent a messenger."

"Some things need to be discussed in person." Henry smiled and took another long draft from his mug.

I watched Robert's eyes carefully dart back and forth between Henry and me while Gerald spoke. It was like he was trying to figure out how it all started, his beginning. I wanted to explain everything to him, especially the heartache I experienced as he was taken from my arms so many years ago, but no words could describe the events of the past.

"Is it true that your nephew, Stephen de Blois, is claiming himself as the next in line for the crown?" I asked.

"Nesta, you are much too interested in politics for a woman," Henry said, and his face flushed but his tone remained flat. "But don't you worry, I don't intend to die any time soon."

"Nesta, I ask you to leave now so we can conduct the King's business in peace," Gerald said pointing toward the exit.

I moved from the room to allow the free speech of the men but stood close enough to hear the conversation.

"I am afraid Nesta was correct, Stephen's activities include convincing the church to endorse him as my successor," Henry said, "but my plan is to install my daughter, Matilda, in case I die before my grandson, Henry II, is of age to take the throne."

"It is a precaution since my father is in good health," Robert said.

"But it does make sense to have an unquestionable plan in place," Gerald said, "but I also agree with Robert that your health is well enough that it will not be an issue."

"I have assigned Robert as Matilda's protector and champion," Henry said.

"A very good choice," Gerald said.

In another life, it would have been my son, Robert, who would be in line for the English throne. He would have brought our two countries peace, but Henry sacrificed that peace and was suffering with his decisions.

"We have come to enlist your support, and if we require forces, you will stand against Stephen," Robert said.

"Of course, you have whatever you need. I am at your service," Gerald said. "The only need I have for any forces is to keep the Welsh at bay."

"That is the other reason we are here—the Welsh have been defeated," Henry said.

"How can you be sure?" Gerald asked.

"Their leader's head was delivered to me only yesterday,"

Henry said.

I held my hand over my mouth, holding in a gasp with tears threatening to fall. I leaned into the wall as my knees weakened.

"Gruffydd?" Gerald asked.

"Gwenllian," Henry said chewing something, "even separated from her body, the woman had the face of an angel."

"Won't that inflame the rebels further?"

"That is why we are here. I need you to confront Gruffydd and make an offer of peace. I will grant him a small piece of land when he swears loyalty to the Crown and pay fealty like his father."

"And if he doesn't agree?"

"Then you will take his life and the life of his children," Henry said still chewing. "I think it is time for you to take your own sons on such a mission of peace."

"My sons are his nephews," Gerald said.

"He will be less likely to kill you on sight, don't you think?"

Gerald stayed silent and at this point, I knew I needed to get word to my brother and beg for peace.

I went to my chamber and wrote a letter to my brother even though I had no idea how I would get it to him before my own husband and sons found him. I was in shock trying not to focus on his grief and the anger he must have had toward the King. I couldn't think of what words should land on the parchment since I felt such hatred for Henry when there was a soft knock on my door.

"Come," I called out, expecting one of my ladies but instead, I turned to see Henry come in and shut the door behind him.

"Henry?"

"My Lady," Henry said, looking like a large dire wolf starved after a long winter.

"My husband and my children are near," I said, backing away as he approached with a wide smile as if my words never reached his ears. When there was no further retreat as my back fell flat against the rail of my own bed, one of Henry's large hands landed firmly on my shoulder as the other expertly pulled the tie at the top of my gown, loosening it until my breasts were fully exposed sending a shiver down my spine.

"It feels like a lifetime ago since my eyes have been filled with such a beautiful sight," Henry said thickly as he leaned into me and put his full mouth around each nipple, one at a time, sucking gently and twirling his tongue in a circular motion finally causing an involuntary stir in my loins.

I let out a small sound which Henry took as a further invitation and he pulled my clothes off my shoulders. The clothes now settled on my hips, exposing my pale stomach with the long thin lines, reminding me of each of my children that had stretched my stomach to its limits, but Henry's tongue found them and simply followed them as paths to where he now knelt, pulling the lace and silk the rest of the way to the floor before bringing his lips so close I could feel his hot breath sending my body into the familiar state whenever Henry was nearby. I watched him touch his own mound, adjusting it from its awkward position.

He rose and easily lifted me to the bed, and in a single movement, had his own trousers off and now pushed himself into me without even a warning. He was so far into me I gasped, causing him to smile as he pushed several times with such solid thrusts it caused the bed to shift. I cried out as if I was pleased and held him tightly, pressing my fingers deep into his skin.

I closed my eyes tight but could smell his breath still fresh with ale and I tried to hold my own breath, waiting for it to end. Finally, his breathing became faster and he released into me with several loud familiar grunts as his movements stopped and he rolled off of me. I lay still, waiting for him to move.

We were silent as we dressed, and as I followed him from my chamber, I saw Gerald standing close as Henry was still adjusting his belt.

"My King," Gerald acknowledged between tight lips.

I stood behind Henry, suddenly afraid as Gerald's face turned bright red and his neck had shrunk into his body. The humiliation that once plagued our marriage had been revived, but Gerald was no longer a young obedient squire but a battle-proven knight bearing not only the scars of war but also the internal wounds that had never healed, festering deep inside his soul.

The rage I saw flash on my husband's face dissipated just as fast, escaping the attention of Henry, or if he noticed, didn't care enough to respond. But I knew the calm that washed over Gerald's face was far more dangerous than the anger. I stayed frozen as Henry confidently moved through the door past Gerald, leaving me exposed.

I hung my head in shame and tried to reach out to my husband, but, with his body stiff, he slapped my hand away. Gerald had never hit me or showed any violence toward me, but I would stay separate in case of a change. Did he think that I had any choice in the King's preferences? If he was standing near enough, he should have realized the noises I made were to lessen the time he had my body, not an indication of pleasure. I wish I could tell my husband that I was also humiliated with no control of this man who used me whenever he wanted. I couldn't tell him I cursed my own womanhood as my body involuntarily responded. I was once a gift to him that wasn't given fully. It wasn't my fault.

My loyalty was to my children as the world has defined my place as less than a man's. Does the cock really define a superior being? Is it that they are so eager to make war and take land? Isn't it a woman who carries the child in her body who produces the male? Why is our worth determined by the blood of our fathers that runs through our veins and not that of our mothers? Gwenllian proved a woman can lead an army and paid the ultimate sacrifice for her people.

I was done with the men in my life dictating my future. I was not going to be their property any longer. I now had a plan to protect my brother and win our land back.

The following day, Gerald sat rigid as I approached him, his lips tight.

"I would like to travel with you to see my brother," I said.

"That is not possible," he said not looking at me. He didn't ask how I knew his mission, but I assumed he no longer cared.

"I am going," I said forcefully, "whether I ride with your contingent or on my own. Don't you think I may have some sway with my brother?"

Gerald stood. "Do what you want," he said as he turned and left the room.

I had my things ready and I rushed to the stables to order my horse readied. I stood adjusting my riding cloak when a large stallion approached. I saw Hait staring down at me.

"You're riding with me, my Lady," he said smiling.

I smiled back warmly. "Am I not the fortunate one today with such protection?"

When the stable boy handed the reins to me, Hait had already left his own horse to help me mount mine.

"Thank you, sir," I said.

"My pleasure," Hait said as he easily mounted his horse and guided me to the waiting party that included my three sons riding with Gerald. I saw that Hait was to keep me situated near the rear, but I wasn't sure if it was for my protection or simply to keep me from Gerald's sight.

We found Gruffydd's camp not even a full day's ride away. The fires were fully lit as the evening was almost upon us. A few scouts had come to greet us but didn't seem alarmed. They must have been forewarned of our peaceful mission. I watched as Gerald greeted my brother in front of the largest tent, and I could see that Gerald was doing all the talking and Gruffydd just stood frozen. I needed to speak to him before he denied the truce.

I waited until Hait was distracted and ran to my brother, surprising both men. I ran into him so hard I almost took him off his feet. As I wrapped my arms around him, I whispered so only he could hear, "Say nothing, we need to talk."

Gruffydd hugged me back hard. Tears fell as I held my

brother. "I'm so sorry," I said through my sobs. I felt Gerald's eyes on me but didn't turn to him. Instead, I kept my focus on my brother and watched a silent tear fall from his eye.

"I need an answer," Gerald spoke behind me.

I released my grip from my brother and turned to Gerald. "Have you no heart?" I screamed.

Gerald looked furious but took a step back where Hait now stood watching the spectacle.

"You have until the morning," Gerald said and then looked at Hait. "Stay with her."

Hait shook his head and we all watched Gerald stomp off.

I looked at Hait with a half-smile and turned to my brother, nodding my head toward the entrance of his tent. I walked in and instantly felt relief. There was a small fire in the center, creating a cloud of smoke lingering above our heads. I sat on a small bench as my brother brought two wooden cups and a cask of ale and sat next to me.

"You have to concede," I said accepting the full cup of ale.

Gruffydd looked at me carefully before speaking. The silence was deafening but I kept my lips sealed, waiting.

"I am surprised at this request," he said softly, "for all the sacrifices we have made to be swept under a mat."

"It's the sacrifices you've made that are the reason for the request," I said.

"Please," he motioned for me to continue.

"The kingdom is divided and promises to get worse. Stephen de Blois is working against Henry's wishes in succession. He believes he is the rightful heir and Henry is determined to make Matilda the lawful heir. He is assuring her succession using Robert as the leader of a large force for assurance. The country is divided as are their resources, and Matilda has her own political motivations in Normandy. She has proposed that Henry turn over the castles in Normandy under her rule before his death. He has denied the request, but the request has stirred a rebellion in Normandy as well and it is rumored Matilda and her husband Geffory are joined in this rebellion. I recognize

Henry's politics and his offer to you is a way to divert his forces now at war with you toward his trouble in Normandy. I feel you could ask for much more if you wanted to."

"Then why wouldn't I ask for more?"

"You will ask for more at the right time," I said quietly, "But you need to be in place in Deheubarth building your alliances for this demand. You must be reinstated as the King of Deheubarth. It is your birthright. You have taken a great loss and I am sure your men want revenge but it is an opportunity that will spare more lives and bring Wales back its independence from the Normans."

"But what of your husband and your children?"

"My husband is of no consequence and my children are grandchildren of a King. They will support their uncle as their leader, as I know your rewards will ensure they will be important men in our history," I said standing.

"I am surprised, sister," he said standing to meet me. "You seem to have it all worked out."

"This will work, Gruffydd, please trust me."

"I trust no one more, sister." Gruffydd hugged me and I held on tight as he kissed the top of my head.

As I opened the flap to exit the tent, my heart leapt from my throat. Standing there was Hait. He reached for my hand and helped me out. How much had he heard? Gruffydd followed me and stood in the front, watching Hait lead me away.

"Hait, I—"

"I'm at your service," he said quietly.

"As Constable to my husband?"

"*Your* service, Nesta," he stopped and looked me straight in the eye, "do you understand?"

"I'm not sure."

"I heard your plan and I will help you achieve your goal."

He must have sensed the confusion on my face because before I could speak, he said, "I can't believe you don't understand how I feel about you, how I've always felt about you."

I stood in shock but smiled at him. "I must also admit that

there has always been a small part of my heart reserved for you but as a protector and as a friend."

"Hopefully, that small piece grows further in the future," he said.

"Do I have a conspirator in my presence?" I asked cocking my head slightly. "Or are you a wickedly confident spy for my husband or the King?"

"I hope I will be able to prove my loyalty to you, Nesta," he bowed low in front of me before walking away. If he was a spy, I would surely hang. If he really was my supporter, I had an un- believable opportunity.

At the evening meal, I sat next to Gerald and told him that I had convinced my brother to accept the King's offer.

"So easily?"

"What else can he do now? He lost his wife and more than half his troops. They are living in tents in the woods. It is an op- portunity to start anew," I said.

"I honestly thought he would be more resistant," Gerald said flatly as he took another bite of his food and washed it down with a deep draft of ale.

The next day we left early morning and I didn't see Gruffydd, but as I rode toward the back of the caravan, Hait told me that the agreement had been made and Gerald would be drawing the transfer papers.

CHAPTER 23

Gerald and I arrived at Henry's court in Westminster with half a dozen men as requested by the King. As always, I was excited to see my sons, Henry and Robert. It had been too long since I had laid my eyes on them.

"I am surprised but delighted Robert is here today," I said. "I was under the impression he hardly left Matilda's side."

"She is recovering from the birth of her second son in Normandy," Hait said. Hait had been by my side since we left South Wales but that wasn't an unusual occurrence anymore. Hait stayed by my side whenever we traveled. Hait's interest in me was more than obvious now but Gerald didn't seem to care. He had become a bitter presence in my life and hardly spoke a word to me or anyone.

"A second son, Henry must be thrilled with Matilda. Henry's line is almost guaranteed to continue. The church can hardly back Stephen's claim now," I said.

"His heir, young Henry is not much more than two years. I think the seat is not yet guaranteed to the lad. It does help sway the Pope by promoting Matilda as the ruler until her son is old enough to sit on the throne," he said.

"Is Stephen no longer a threat?" I asked

"I feel he will always be a threat until the Pope declares succession. But now the country is at peace," Hait told me.

Finding Henry not in attendance instantly changed Gerald's disposition. He unclenched his jaw and I even caught a rare smile as he spoke with his kinsman at the gathering. Since the last time Henry visited Carew, Gerald wore his resentment in plain sight, and anyone who knew him knew he was weighed down over the past few years, except for Henry, who was oblivious and didn't understand that he was the source of Gerald's demeanor. Henry has always lived in his own world; his wants and needs were of the highest priority, and he knew how to achieve those goals he set upon.

"Good day, my Ladies and Lords," Robert's voice boomed, quieting the small crowd that had been summoned. "I am speaking for the King today, who unfortunately had a last-minute engagement."

The crowd rumbled quietly, each guessing the "type" of engagement the King would have more important than addressing the crowd he himself had assembled. I heard murmurs of "he never let anything come before a beautiful woman in his bed" and "he is busy counting his silver," and "he has been ill."

Robert interrupted the low-leveled gossip with a loud clearing of his throat. I watched him as he represented his father not only in word but in action. The way he moved his arms and shifted his feet as he spoke, he was the image of the King but not the King he now represented. He reminded me of my own father in looks but in another life, as Henry's firstborn, his name should be on the succession decree. But that was not how history would show and my son held his loyalty close to his sister. The part of his father that would murder his own brother didn't exist in the man that stood tall in front of us. His loyalty was well placed as it would maintain peace.

"The threat of the crown has been diminished as Stephen has placed an oath to concede the throne to Matilda. Finally, the country will know peace within its borders," Robert announced, causing the crowd to break into cheers. The supporters of Henry were all concerned if Stephen was to assume the crown. The church would have more power and take more land for their cathedrals, increasing taxes as a result.

I looked across the crowd and found my brother's face. He caught my glance and I could tell the news was worse for him than for me, but I vowed silently and he understood that I would see to it that he was restored as the rightful Welsh King.

Later in the day, I found Martha, the young Welsh girl, now a woman, I once relied on for information.

"Welcome back, my Lady," she said.

"Martha, I am desperate for your help," I said. "Is the news of Stephen's ambitions to the crown not well known?"

"Not that I know, my Lady, but I can tell you the health of the King is suffering," she said in a whisper.

"What do you mean?"

"It is his heart that gives him trouble. Each episode lasting a little longer than the last," she said.

"Where is he now?" I asked.

"He is in his bed but it is a closely held secret, with only the closest and most trustworthy household staff to aid him during his confinements."

"Rumors of a sick king could cause unwanted speculation and unrest in the kingdom."

"Exactly," she said.

"Don't tell anyone we spoke," I said.

"Remember, my Lady, I am a Welshwoman and true to my people," she said.

"I know you are," I said reaching out and hugging her, which took her by surprise.

Henry showed his face the next day. I could tell he looked thin and a bit tired, but to most people, he looked perfectly normal.

"In celebration of peace once again in our country, I will be traveling to Lyons-la-Foret to welcome my second grandson, second heir to the throne," he said to the crowd, which cheered.

"He wants us to believe him a caring grandfather but I have it on authority that his goal is to put an end to it Matilda's ambitions to rule Normandy," Hait said.

"Will you go with him?" I asked.

"He has invited me, as well as your husband," Hait said "Since the trip is masked as a celebration, there will be a hunt and a great feast in honor of the new child."

"Do you love me?" I asked, facing Hait.

"You know I love you; I am fully devoted to you," he said melting in front of me.

"Well, I plan to test that devotion," I said looking around for any ears that might be close. "Henry has controlled my life for too long. He treats me like I am his personal property and he has only released a small piece of land to Gruffydd instead of his full birthright."

"I understand, but what can we do?" he asked, also looking around to make sure we were not being overheard.

"Henry is not well," I said. "The household staff keeps the information close as to not ignite a civil war. I have a plan but I need you to accept the King's invitation and convince Gerald to come with you. I will tell you the rest of the plan if it comes together."

"Please be careful, Nesta," he said and I kissed his cheek causing him to blush.

"I plan on it," I said as I walked away to go find Martha.

A few days later, the ship was being loaded and the men were making final preparations. Henry seemed to be in a good mood as he greeted all his companions as they boarded the vessel. I was standing at the end of the pier when Gerald and Hait arrived carrying their chests.

"My Lady," Hait acknowledged me.

"I am surprised at the send-off," Gerald said.

"I've brought you a send-off package," I said, handing Gerald a basket full of some of his favorite treats, including dried apples and walnuts baked into sweet bread, and then handed Hait a similar basket. Gerald took the basket without a word and headed to the ship, leaving Hait alone with me.

"Here is your send-off," I said. "Don't open it yet, but near the bottom are two small lampreys wrapped tightly as not to broadcast the smell. There is a bucket of live lampreys that was loaded for the feast in two days. I need you to place the two I put here into the bucket before they cook them up. By time the cooks get a hold of the bucket, the live ones will be slow or still, so hopefully they won't notice the bad ones floating in a full bucket."

"What if someone else eats the fish?"

"They won't. No one dares to eat one of Henry's favorite meals," I said. "He has them prepared complete and prefers to divide them himself as he devours them. He takes great pleasure watching others wince as he sucks out each eye. It is not pleasant to watch, I assure you."

"I will do what I can," he said touching my shoulder before turning and walking to the ship.

I stood in place, watching the large ship float into the center of the English Channel, headed out under the gloom of this late November day. I waved to no one in particular but as I did, it felt symbolic as if I were waving goodbye to the past. Hopefully, when I arrived home, Gruffydd would have good news.

I reached Deheubarth several days ahead of Gruffydd and could not concentrate on anything. When he finally crossed the bridge and I could see his face, he didn't have to utter a word. Henry's nephew, Stephen de Blois, had agreed to reinstate Gruffydd as the King of Deheubarth, and Gruffydd vowed to support the new King with arms and finances, defending his throne against Matilda.

It was the second week of December when Hait finally arrived back to Deheubarth. I ran to the courtyard as soon as I heard the bell. I knew it had to be news, good or bad.

"The King is dead," Hait said before he even dismounted.

"How?" I asked hoping it was my actions that caused his last breath.

"It's recorded as a bad case of food poisoning, and with his recent heart trouble, he didn't recover," he said.

"I am sorry for you to be dragged into my conspiracy, but I am glad he is dead," I said but as I spoke the words, I did feel a piece of my heart hurt just a bit.

"Let's never speak of it again," he said.

"I missed you so," I said giving Hait just enough permission that he wrapped his arms around me and held me tight. I took his affection willingly and let my body relax in his strength until I noticed the absence of Gerald.

"Where is Gerald?" I asked Hait with my face still buried in his chest.

"Gerald is dead," he said letting his arms relax enough that I could push away and look him directly in the eye.

"How?"

"It was a robbery," he said.

He motioned to the horses. I was so excited for the news of the King, I hadn't noticed that Hait was leading a horse with no rider but it wasn't just any horse, it was the familiar black stallion Gerald was so proud of. It also wasn't without a rider. Gerald's body was draped sideways across the horse's back.

"Gerald's dead," I said staring at the lifeless body.

"I'm so sorry," he said. I searched his eyes, confused before I sank to the ground.

"I'm free," I said in a whisper that Hait couldn't hear.

"Are you okay?" Hait sat on the cold ground next to me.

"I don't understand," I said, allowing tears to fall. I had steadied myself for Henry's death and justified it as necessary to reinstate Wales to its rightful rule, but Gerald had been my husband for so many years and I never imagined him gone. My emotions were mixed.

"How did it happen?"

"We came to rest for the evening in the forest at Wygall. Gerald stayed to build a fire while I fetched water from a nearby stream. It was dusk and I was lucky to find two rabbits foraging nearby, so I took a little longer away from camp than I would have. I was eager to see the look on Gerald's face when I brought back fresh rabbit in the middle of winter, but when I returned, I witnessed two woodsmen struggling on the ground with Gerald. As soon as they spotted me, they jumped off Gerald and disappeared into the woods. I ran to Gerald and found his own dagger thrust deep into his heart. There was nothing I could do but hold his head as his life slowly slipped away."

"Why were you two alone? Where were all your men?"

"We left them in London with Robert to support Matilda. As soon as Henry's death was announced, Stephen was across the Channel and had already taken control of England. He is supported by the church and making the claim to the people that only he could provide order at a critical time. His previous oath to Henry in support of Matilda was made before the country was in the hands of a two-year-old boy. The Welsh have already pledged their support and the Scotts are said to also be in favor of Stephen."

My tears stopped and I stood with Hait's strong arms supporting me. I felt weak and strong at the same time. After all, this turn of events was initiated by me, actions set right for the mistakes I made so long ago. I searched my heart for regret and found none, but then I turned to face Hait.

"Where are the rabbits?"

Printed in Great Britain
by Amazon

69733313R00116